Jade stared at Father Christmas

Horrified, she noticed that her slap had knocked his white beard askew.

Before she could say a word, Father Christmas had burst into speech. "She slapped my face, Pen!" he told the other woman standing there, before once again giving that triumphant laugh.

Jade looked from Penny to her husband, Simon, wondering why one of them didn't slap Father Christmas's face again—this time for hysteria. But the couple just looked on bemusedly.

This time Jade caught the side of his eye—which only seemed to fuel his excitement. "My God, Penny, Simon," he cried. "Do you realize what this means?" Jade had more than a good idea: the man was ever so slightly insane. "I was attracted to her on sight," Father Christmas was rambling on. "But now I know I'm going to marry her!"

CAROLE MORTIMER, one of our most popular—and prolific—English authors, began writing in the Harlequin Presents series in 1979. She now has more than forty top-selling romances to her credit and shows no sign whatever of running out of plot ideas. She writes strong traditional romances with a distinctly modern appeal, and her winning way with characters and romantic plot twists has earned her an enthusiastic audience worldwide.

Books by Carole Mortimer

Don't miss any of our special offers. Write to us at the following address for information on our newest releases.

Harlequin Reader Service
901 Fuhrmann Blvd., P.O. Box 1397, Buffalo, NY 14240
Canadian address: P.O. Box 603,
Fort Erie, Ont. L2A 5X3

CAROLE MORTIMER

the loving gift

Harlequin Books

TORONTO • NEW YORK • LONDON
AMSTERDAM • PARIS • SYDNEY • HAMBURG
STOCKHOLM • ATHENS • TOKYO • MILAN

For
Matthew and Joshua

Harlequin Presents first edition December 1989
ISBN 0-373-11227-0

Original hardcover edition published in 1988
by Mills & Boon Limited

CHAPTER ONE

'Yo HO HO! Yo ho ho! Merry Christmas! *Merry Christmas!*' boomed the tall, rounded figure in the unmistakable red suit as he ambled into the room, the obligatory sack of toys thrown over one broad shoulder. 'Have you all been good boys and girls this year?'

The loud cries of 'Yes!' from the hundred and fifty children who filled the room, that instantly followed the teasing question, almost drowned out the gasp of stunned surprise made by the woman standing at Jade's side but, completely attuned herself to any minor or major disaster that might befall any of the pupils at what had so far been a very successful preparatory school Christmas party, Jade was instantly alerted by Penny's sudden tension.

Jade anxiously surveyed the room, seeing only the excited faces of the children as they eagerly awaited the calling of their name to go up and collect their present from Father Christmas, most of them lingering to tell him what they would like on Christmas night.

She turned back to Penny with puzzled eyes, her concern deepening when she saw how ashen-faced the other woman had become. And Penny's attention seemed to be focused on the jolly Father

7

Christmas as he happily distributed the carefully chosen presents to each child. Which was all the more surprising, considering that the man behind the flowing white beard and artificially glowing red cheeks was, in fact, Penny's own husband!

The only reason Jade could even imagine for Penny's behaviour was if the Father Christmas disguise had come astray and revealed to the totally enrapt audience that only a mere man lay beneath it, and that man was their own headmaster. But the wig and false beard were firmly in place, the rouge unsmudged on the padded cheeks, and the pillow beneath the red coat and wide black belt hadn't slipped an inch since Simon had got himself ready half an hour earlier.

Then what was bothering Penny? Because something certainly was as she took over the task of organising each child going up to collect their gift, her dazed gaze more often than not fixed on 'Father Christmas' as he enthusiastically distributed the gaily wrapped parcels.

Jade didn't find an opportunity to talk to the other woman for some time. 'Penny——'

'And who is this last little girl we have over here?' boomed that overly jocular voice of 'Father Christmas' with lilting emphasis.

'Penny, what——' The sudden silence that had fallen over the room, quickly followed by childish giggles, halted Jade in mid-flow, and she slowly turned her attention back into the spacious hall that had housed the Christmas party.

One hundred and fifty—one hundred and fifty-*one*, pairs of eyes were riveted on her, one hundred and fifty of them with laughing expectation, the hundred and fifty-first pair glinting with mocking blue humour.

'What would you like me to bring *you* on Christmas night?' Father Christmas/Simon prompted huskily.

'Oh, God,' Penny muttered weakly at Jade's side.

Oh, God, indeed. Simon had to have been at the sherry he always kept locked away in his office, for visiting parents, to be acting in this outrageous manner. Maybe Simon's role as Father Christmas *was* the reason Penny was looking so stricken. Jade had never seen Simon partake of more than one polite glass of sherry at one time, with no effect on him whatsoever, but Penny was obviously deeply concerned by his behaviour now—and with good reason.

'What's your name, little girl?' he prompted persistently, and the titters from the watching children increased.

Jade's mouth pursed disapprovingly. Penny and Simon had been very kind to her since she had begun working for them on a temporary basis at the beginning of the winter term, but Simon's drawing attention to her, and himself, in this way, was totally uncalled for. Maybe Simon was one of those worst of things, an unpleasant drunk. Although at the moment his eyes merely glittered with devilish humour.

'Come and sit on Santa's knee and tell me your deepest desire—for Christmas,' that teasingly provocative voice encouraged again.

Jade felt really uncomfortable now, her cheeks fiery red as she knew she was what she seemed to be: the centre of attention, the other members of staff deeply amused by this unexpected turn of events, the children fascinated by the show. And if there was one thing Jade hated it was to be the cynosure of all eyes.

She plastered a polite smile on suddenly stiff lips, green eyes flashing warningly. Not that Father Christmas—Simon—seemed to be at all deterred by her ferocity, his grin widening wickedly. Good grief, how much of the sherry had he had?

'Come on, little girl,' he provoked. 'Don't you realise how busy I am at this time of year?'

Not too busy that he couldn't spare a few minutes to guzzle down what appeared to be a bottle of sherry! 'I appreciate that—Father Christmas,' she spoke softly, huskily, her natural tone, a voice that her young pupils listened to with eagerness, and which few other people took note of. Although at the moment that certainly wasn't the case! 'Which is why we really mustn't keep you any longer,' she dismissed with bright lightness.

'Oh, I have more than enough time to listen to what you would like to be waiting for you at the foot of your bed on Christmas morning,' he drawled mockingly.

Jade didn't know how to cope with this situation any longer, turning desperately to Penny, dismayed to see that the other woman was still completely speechless. If it wasn't for the fact that approximately one hundred and fifty children were watching the exchange, the incident would have been relatively easy to deal with—but one just didn't go around punching Father Christmas on the chin in front of so many starry eyes! Instead she had to settle for what she hoped would be a verbal dressing-down.

'The space at the foot of my bed is already firmly occupied,' she bit out quietly, green eyes flashing with unaccustomed irritation. She absolutely hated having this attention drawn to her! 'So I think I'll give any gifts you might have in mind for me a miss this year, thank you.'

The Father Christmas was shaking his head even as she spoke. 'Father Christmas has to bring you *something*—doesn't he, children?' he boomingly encouraged their involvement in the conversation.

The excited cries of 'Yes!' filled the room once more.

His persistence was unnerving, and Jade once again turned to Penny, only to find that the other woman had now gone a ghostly white. Which wasn't surprising!

Penny's young sister Cathy had been a friend of Jade's since college, and when she had told Jade about the temporary post at this private preparatory school it had been convenient for all of them that Jade was able to fill in until the usual teacher of the reception class returned from maternity leave at Easter.

The last three months had been rewarding both professionally and personally for Jade, and until this moment she hadn't had reason to regret her move from her London home to a rented cottage in Devon. Now she was beginning to wonder if it might not have been better for all of them if Cathy had never mentioned the vacancy to her—it was a sure fact that there would be repercussions from this incident, if only personally.

Jade gave a tight smile. 'I'll make you up a list when I have more time,' she dismissed curtly. 'Right now we have to prepare the children for going home,' she added briskly. 'We——'

'Oh, surely you can spare just a few minutes to whisper a little something in my ear?' 'Father Christmas' moved agilely across the room to her side—much more agilely than the true bulk could possibly have allowed!—his arm moving strongly about her waist as he pulled her firmly up against him, the twinkle in the blue eyes definitely lecherous now. 'Come on now, sweetheart.' He bent down to her much shorter height. 'Tell me what you would like me to bring you.'

No Father Christmas—and especially a married one!—had any right to be talking to her in this flirtatious way!

Jade gave a furious sigh as she moved closer to the wig-covered ear nearest to her. 'I'd like to take away the key to your drinks cabinet and throw it in the village pond,' she muttered, all the time smiling brightly for their audience, although she could see her colleagues—the braver ones, at least!—were having trouble controlling their mirth now. Ordinarily Jade would have been one of the first to laugh at herself, but not when she was being made a spectacle of.

Blue eyes gleamed wickedly as he moved back slightly to look down at her. 'Really?' he drawled mockingly. 'That wouldn't do you too much good at the moment—the village pond is frozen over!'

She glared. 'Perhaps a little icy air might do *you* some good just now!'

'Oh, I doubt it,' he taunted. 'Father Christmas isn't too bothered about the cold.'

'Only by too much alcohol, obviously,' she returned tartly in a fierce whisper.

He feigned hurt surprise. 'I haven't touched a drop since——'

'At the most half an hour ago,' Jade scorned, feeling deeply for Penny during this embarrassing display. How uncomfortable the other woman must feel at the exchange. And, even allowing for 'Christmas spirit', it was going to be difficult for them all to work together after this; it had gone far beyond the realms of a practical joke.

'Father Christmas' shrugged. 'I may have had a little nip of brandy to keep out the cold——'

'I thought you said Father Christmas wasn't affected by the cold,' she reminded tartly.

'I'm not,' he grinned. 'Not once I've had my nip of brandy!'

She frowned. 'Simon——'

'My, that's quite a list you have there once you got going,' he said loudly enough for their audience to hear, smiling jovially at them all. 'Anything else?' he encouraged brightly.

Considering that she was normally a non-violent person, Jade had an unaccountable urge to hit him! 'I want you to stop this right now,' she grated between clenched teeth.

'Why?' he taunted unconcernedly. 'I'm thoroughly enjoying myself.'

'I'm glad one of us is!' She tried to move away from his arm about her waist and suddenly discovered he was much stronger than he looked in the loose-fitting tweed jacket and plain trousers that were his everyday garb. 'You're going to regret this in the morning,' she warned with impatient rebuke.

'What's that saying?' he grinned. ' "Tomorrow never comes"?'

She chanced a glance at Penny's ashen face. 'Oh, I think it might do for you,' she muttered.

He turned to give the other woman a considering look. 'Hm, Penny does look a little green around the edges,' he mused. 'Maybe I should ask her what she would like on her bed Christmas morning?'

'A sober husband, I should think,' Jade bit out angrily, having found it was impossible to escape that confining arm about her waist—and goodness knew, without being too obvious, she had tried!

Blue eyes gleamed wickedly once again. 'Maybe you would be interested in listening to what I'd like in my bed on Christmas——'

'I don't think so,' she interrupted quickly, unnerved by this streak of flirtation with danger that she had never guessed existed inside a man who, while full of good humour, never failed to be thoughtfully kind.

'Perhaps not,' he lightly accepted her rebuke. 'We wouldn't want to be overheard.'

'*We* have already made enough of a spectacle of ourselves,' she cut in abruptly, grateful to see that Penny at least seemed to be coming out of her daze, some of the colour back in her cheeks as she began to organise the children's home-going, at the same time providing an adequate diversion from what had been proving to be very entertaining for their avid audience; some of their colleagues even looked slightly disappointed that they were obviously going to miss Simon's imminent dressing-down, Penny obviously intending to wait until they were alone before tackling him.

'Talking of spectacles, are yours really necessary?' he took advantage of the noisy organisation around them to whisper seductively in her ear. 'Or are they just a deterrent against interested males?'

'If they are, they aren't working!' she snapped, her eyes flashing darkly, annoyed that he should have guessed that she really only needed the glasses for reading but chose to wear them constantly.

'And your hair.' He looked at her consideringly. 'I bet it looks very sexy when it's left free about your shoulders.'

She drew in an impatient sigh. 'My hair happens to be a frizzy mess when not kept in this style,' she claimed defensively, irritated that he should find anything wrong with the neat coil she always wore

about the crown of her head. She had always worn
her hair like this when she was working, although
she had to admit it had perhaps become a little more
severe lately...

He continued to look at her questioningly. 'I
refuse to believe those silken-looking tresses could
ever be a frizzy mop,' he finally decided.

'Believe what you want.' Her cheeks still burnt
from the lie. 'But for goodness' sake pull yourself
together and start acting like the headmaster you
are.' She looked about them again uncomfortably,
feeling guilty for not joining in the preparations for
home-time, but if she should leave Simon to his
own devices now, heaven knew what he would do
next!

'I am?' He frowned vaguely. 'Oh, yes,' he
grinned. 'For a moment there I almost thought I
was Father Christmas. I know there are several
things I would like to give you that——'

'Oh, for goodness' sake!' Jade rolled her eyes
heavenwards. 'I hope Penny gives you hell for this,'
she muttered.

He turned to smile indulgently at Penny as she
helped some of the younger children put on their
coats. 'She probably will,' he acknowledged
philosophically.

Jade wasn't feeling quite so hot now that they
were no longer the centre of attention, although
there was still the problem of how they were to face
each other again after the holidays. Or how she was
going to face Penny! The poor woman must feel
devastated by Simon's behaviour.

'You should be ashamed of yourself,' Jade told the man at her side emotionally.

'I probably will be later,' he shrugged unconcernedly. 'Right now I'm enjoying myself too much to feel anything else.'

Who would have believed that the gentle giant of a man whom all the children loved and respected so much could possibly behave in this outrageous fashion?

'Well, you'll have to go on enjoying yourself without me.' Jade felt no compunction about putting him down now that there was activity and noise about them. 'I have work to do,' she dismissed firmly.

'And you think I haven't?' he returned in a pained voice. 'What about all those toys I have to finish by next week? The reindeer to feed and water? The——'

'Simon, for heaven's sake,' she sighed her impatience. 'Why don't you just take yourself off to your office and sober up? We can cope with anything that comes up here.'

Laughter gleamed mockingly in his eyes. 'I'm sure you can; you, especially, seem more than capable. But don't you think I should wave goodbye to all the children as they leave?'

The children would probably love it, but would *he* behave long enough to complete the task without mishap?

'I promise I will,' he chuckled softly at her side, causing Jade to turn to him sharply.

'If you can read my mind that well, you know what I'm thinking right now,' she flashed.

'I do indeed,' he drawled. 'But you're asking the impossible.'

Her eyes widened. 'I am?'

'Hm,' he nodded. 'A thousand miles between us couldn't possibly change the way I react to that clear green of your eyes, how I want to release your hair and run my fingers——'

'Please!' Jade snapped agitatedly, moving abruptly away from him. She was well aware of the fact that an excess of alcohol was supposed to loosen the tongue, but this was ridiculous! Surely Simon hadn't always felt this way about her? It certainly hadn't been apparent from his almost fatherly concern for her to date.

'You're right,' he said briskly, drawing himself up to his full padded height of over six feet. 'The children must come first. We can continue this interesting conversation once they've gone.'

If Jade had her way she would be long gone from here before Simon found her again. And, once on her own, she would have to give serious thought as to what was going to happen next term. She couldn't just walk out on her job, she refused to let people down in that way, also knowing it would be confusing for the children in her class to have yet another change of teacher. Damn Simon for indulging in his secret vice when he should have been preparing for his role as Father Christmas!

She looked on a little dazedly as, walking away from her, he fell easily into playing his seasonal role, his booming voice calling out good wishes to the children as he was surrounded by them as they went outside.

Jade's legs felt weak, and instead of joining in the revelry outside she sank weakly down into a nearby chair.

She *liked* working at the Kendrick Preparatory School, and after only one term of being here she was disappointed that it wasn't to be a permanent position. She even liked living in this small Devonshire village, where she was on a first-name basis with all her delivery men. And after living in town all of her life, the last four years of that in London in an apartment on her own, where she had to go out to the shops to buy all her needs, she hadn't expected to adapt so readily to country life. She willingly admitted that it had been the warm hospitality she had received from Penny and Simon that had helped ease her into this totally different way of life.

Penny, loving Simon as she undoubtedly did, couldn't be blamed for thinking Jade must have encouraged Simon's behaviour of a few minutes ago in some way. She couldn't possibly be expected to believe—as Jade herself found it difficult to!—that her mild-mannered husband could behave so recklessly without encouragement of some sort, even with the artificial confidence of alcohol.

It all had such repercussive consequences, also endangering Jade's long-standing friendship with Cathy, the other woman having no choice but to side with her sister. And she had even tentatively been looking forward to Christmas among her new friends. She had been invited to several functions at Penny and Simon's over the holiday period, their two children home for the holidays to complete the family unit. Cathy would also be trying to come down for a few days later on. Now all of that looked very precarious, although at this moment a long and lonely festive season seemed the least of her worries; her job was in jeopardy, a job that meant more to her than any of the people here could realise.

'Would you like to start clearing up the mess?'

Jade gave a guilty start as she looked up at Penny, feeling ill at how pale and exhausted the other woman looked. 'Penny, about what happened earlier——' she began awkwardly.

'Yes. I—I'm sorry about that,' Penny answered vaguely, not at all her usual authoritative self—and who could blame her? 'I—could you and the others tidy up here?' She looked uncertainly at the debris in the room from the end-of-term party. 'I have to go and look for Simon,' she added agitatedly.

Jade gave a pained frown. 'I just want to try and explain—— '

'Could we talk later?' Penny's voice was sharp; a small, pretty, blonde woman, slightly overweight, and looking all the more attractive because of that, she possessed the sort of organising mind that more or less kept the school running on a day-to-day basis. 'I really do need to find Simon,' she frowned.

That shouldn't be too difficult: she just had to follow the sound of the booming 'Yo ho hos'!

'I quite understand.' Jade nodded heavily. 'But I do need to talk to you afterwards,' she added firmly.

'Of course.' The other woman nodded, her mind obviously elsewhere. 'I'll just go and find Simon,' she repeated distantly before disappearing out of the room in search of her husband.

Jade felt even more deflated than she had before; despite her reluctance to discuss it now, Penny was obviously deeply disturbed by Simon's behaviour. But weren't they all? At least none of the children had guessed that 'Father Christmas' was more than a little inebriated. But it would only need one of the pupils to mention to their parents Father Christmas's more than seasonal familiarity with one of the teachers for more than Simon's relationship with Penny to be in jeopardy; most of those parents were well aware of the fact that Simon annually took the part of Father Christmas!

The Kendrick school was one of the best of its kind in the country, and Jade had instantly felt comfortable and at ease working in such a happy and contented atmosphere. It wouldn't remain that way for long if people were to learn that Simon took the occasional secret tipple. He risked so much for what appeared to be no more than a craving for something that completely changed his personality—and not for the better!

But Jade put a brave face on the incident when the others returned from outside—Penny and 'Father Christmas' conspicuous in their absence— as she helped to organise the clearing-up process, relieved when the only thing left to do was clear away the carol books in a cupboard. She smiled as she thought of the angelic faces of the children as they had all gathered around the piano to sing Christmas carols beside the flamboyantly decorated tree, each child having made at least one decoration to adorn it. There was something so magical about the innocence of children at this time of year, and it was virtually impossible not to feel drawn into the fantasy.

'Dare I hope that at least part of that smile is for me?'

Jade spun around with a start, disconcerted to suddenly find herself face to face with 'Father Christmas' once more. And he didn't look in the least repentant!

'Penny was looking for you,' she told him sharply, watching him warily.

He nodded, taking up most of the doorway to the store-cupboard. 'She found me,' he drawled.

Her frown turned to puzzlement; if Penny had managed to locate him, what on earth was he doing wandering around loose again in his condition? 'You haven't upset Penny again, have you?' she asked suspiciously.

He shrugged. 'She was crying her eyes out when I left her just now.'

Green eyes widened incredulously. 'And you just *left* her?'

'Well—not exactly. But I needed to see you again before you went home,' he excused himself.

'Penny—was—crying—her—eyes—out—and—
you—just——!' Jade's incredulity turned to disgust
as she stared at him in disbelief.

'I told you, I needed to see you before you left,'
he insisted.

'To apologise?' Her eyes flashed warningly at his
utter selfishness.

He did manage to look a little shame-faced. 'I
suppose I did go a little over the top a short while
ago, but I was only——'

'Over the top?' Jade repeated with soft anger.
'You were utterly outrageous!'

He grinned. 'I don't normally act in that impetuous way, it's just that——'

'I'm well aware of the way you *normally* act,'
she snapped, wishing she could have the usual
Simon back again, instead of this virtual stranger.

'—I was attracted to you the moment I entered
the room,' he concluded as if she hadn't interrupted so vehemently.

'That you were——! My God, Simon!' Jade
choked emotionally. 'You've really gone too far
now. That scene you created a little while ago I
could maybe excuse because of the amount of alcohol you've apparently consumed, but to come
here to me now, when Penny is obviously broken-
hearted, is inexcusable.'

'I was only——'

'Don't you dare touch me!' she warned harshly
as he would have reached out for her.

'But I——'

'Don't say I didn't warn you!' she choked at the same time as her hand made contact with the side of his face in a resounding slap.

Jade stared at him in horror after the uncharacteristic violence—and then she swayed dizzily as he began to laugh, a loudly triumphant laugh that convinced her he wasn't drunk, after all, but bordering on the insane! The strain of owning and running the school must have become too much for him. No one in their right mind *laughed* when they had been slapped the way he just had!

And then her own horror turned to a pained groan as Penny suddenly appeared in the doorway. She was terrified that the other woman would actually think she had been encouraging Simon in this madness. 'Penny, I'm so sorry about all this, but I——'

'You have no reason to be sorry about anything,' the other woman dismissed easily, gazing affectionately at the man in the Father Christmas suit as he still grinned idiotically, the only sign of her recent tears a slight puffiness about her eyes. 'He always did have a warped sense of humour,' she excused him indulgently.

Jade had never noticed it before! 'I still wouldn't want you to think that I encouraged him,' she insisted pleadingly.

Penny smiled. 'I'm sure he didn't need encouraging.' She shook her head.

It was wonderful that Penny could take her husband's errant behaviour in her stride—Jade wished she could come to terms with it as easily!

'You really are incorrigible.' Penny shook her head with rueful disapproval at the grinning 'Father Christmas'. 'If you have——'

'Darling, surely there has to be a better place for this conversation than a store-cupboard?' Simon chided lightly as he appeared in the doorway behind his wife—wearing his usual school attire of tweed jacket and tailored trousers.

Jade froze as she stared at him, turning slowly to face the man in the Father Christmas suit. If it wasn't Simon—and she knew now without a doubt that it wasn't!—then who *was* he?

CHAPTER TWO

'I'M TELLING you, Wellington, *he* almost met his Waterloo after that stupid stunt,' Jade muttered as she poured the cream from the top of her milk into a saucer, giving a snort of disgust as the cat merely looked up at her with pitying eyes before turning his attention to the treat she had put down in front of him.

Jade watched the avid lapping of that delicate pink tongue for several seconds; Wellington certainly had the right idea, concentrating on his drink to the exclusion of all else certainly beat working yourself up into a temper because of the stupidity of some totally insensitive man!

Wellington had appeared on the doorstep of her rented cottage only her second day here, immediately earning his name, completely snowy white except for the four totally black feet that gave him the appearance of wearing wellington boots.

In the beginning Jade had assumed the friendly cat had wandered over from one of the cottages close by, but after several days of returning home to find him sitting on the doorstep waiting for her she had found out from a neighbour that the cat belonged to no one, that the old lady who had once owned him had died some time ago and the cat hadn't let anyone near him since then, living wild.

Two strays together, Jade had thought ruefully. Whether he had sensed some need in her that matched his own, or whether he had just decided she looked soft-hearted enough to feed him without demanding too much in return, she didn't know. But, whatever the reason, he had made the cottage his home the last few months, and when the time came for Jade to leave she didn't know what she was going to do about him. Wellington had become her constant companion, her confidant, someone she could talk to without fear of judgement or re-buttal, and she believed that in his own feline way he had come to care for her too, curling up to sleep on the foot of her bed every night, like a sentinel on guard. But at the same time she knew she couldn't take him back to be cooped up in her rented apartment in London, and there was no way she could afford to buy a house of her own out of town.

But there could be no doubt that Wellington had attached himself to her, and she to him.

His drink finished to his satisfaction, he now strolled across to stretch himself out in front of the fire Jade had lit when she came in, proceeding to wash himself with leisurely strokes of his tongue, pausing in the task to look up at her enquiringly as he sensed her gaze upon him.

She quirked mocking brows. 'So, you're finally ready to listen now, are you?' she derided, putting the milk bottle away in the fridge before joining the cat in front of the fire, taking with her the cup of tea she had just poured for herself, knowing she had been right about his readiness to listen to her now as he contentedly began to wash again. 'You're very definite about your priorities, aren't you, boy?' she teased, absently stroking that silky fur, receiving a rasp of the pink tongue over her hand for her trouble.

She leant back against a chair, giving a pained sigh. 'I have had the most awful afternoon, Wellington.' She shook her head, thinking back to what had transpired after Simon had interrupted that conversation in the store-cupboard.

She had stared at 'Father Christmas' with wide, horrified eyes, noticing as she did so that her slap to the side of his face had knocked the flowing white beard slightly askew, some of it having parted with his cheek completely, revealing a face that, although very similar to Simon's in features, was obviously younger than the other man's, something that was unmistakable now that his face was more fully revealed.

Before she could say a word, 'Father Christmas' had burst into speech. 'She slapped my face, Pen!' he told the other woman excitedly before once again giving that triumphant laugh. And he didn't seem able to stop.

Jade looked from Penny to Simon, wondering why one of them didn't step forward and slap 'Father Christmas's' face again—this time for hysteria. But the couple just looked on bemusedly, and so it was left to Jade to take the initiative before the whole thing turned into more of a farce than it already was.

Because her victim was more of a moving target this time, her aim wasn't quite so good, and instead of making contact with the man's cheek she caught the side of his eye. To her horror, this only seemed to fuel his excitement!

'My God, I'll probably have a black eye from that one,' he cried excitedly. 'Penny, Simon, do you realise what this means?'

Jade had more than a good idea; the man behind the Father Christmas suit was ever so slightly insane. No one in their right mind could possibly be *pleased* at having their face slapped, not once but twice! This man's disturbed state of mind might also explain Penny's ashen face when she had realised it wasn't her husband beneath the disguise, for it was obvious now that that was the reason Penny had looked so distressed when 'Father Christmas' came into the room. Simon, she could see at a glance, was as sober as he always was.

'I was attracted to her on sight,' 'Father Christmas' was rambling on. 'But now I know I'm going to marry her!'

Marry her? The man was definitely certifiable!

Penny was the first one to recover her voice. 'David, can't you see you're distressing her?' she soothed. 'Jade isn't used to—no woman is, I'm sure——' she added with brisk dismissal '—to six foot two Father Christmases proposing marriage to her at their first meeting!'

David. At least she could put a name to the man now, and from the similarity between him and Simon she would say his surname was Kendrick.

David Kendrick. No wonder Simon had never spoken of having a brother; David was definitely the 'black sheep' of the family!

And, if anything, Penny was understating her reaction to David's claim that he was going to marry her; she was more convinced than ever that the man in the Father Christmas suit was in need of medical help!

'But, Penny, can't you see it's like a sign?' he was insisting now. 'And she didn't just slap me once, but twice!'

Penny eyed Jade uncertainly, obviously alarmed by the pallor of her cheeks. 'David, I don't think you should persist in this just now.'

Jade had had enough, couldn't take any more today. 'I think I should be going now, Penny——'

'You can't go!' David pounced, grabbing both her hands in his, holding her captive. 'I've only just found you—do you have any idea how long I've been waiting for you to come into my life?' he prompted eagerly, continuing to talk before she could even attempt an answer to his question. 'Do you think I'm going to let you walk away from me now, when all I know about you is that your name is Jade and you're great with kids?'

And that he intended marrying her. Incredible, absolutely incredible. And the day had progressed so normally until his advent into her life, too!

'David, I really think it might be better to leave this just now,' Penny intervened again, shooting Jade nervous glances.

'But I can't,' he insistently refused, keeping a firm grip on Jade's hands. 'It's like a sign, Penny,' he repeated firmly. 'A blessing——'

'If I read all the signs correctly just now, Jade is getting ready to shout "escaped lunatic"!' Penny stepped forward to pointedly release Jade from the steely grasp. 'David, there has to be a better place and time for this,' she told him firmly.

'The poor girl will come to no other conclusion than that you have a few screws loose if you continue to talk in this way,' Simon put in softly.

If he continued...? Jade was already *convinced* the man had a serious problem!

David looked perplexed. 'But you both know the significance——'

'Yes, yes,' Penny quickly silenced him, shooting Jade an embarrassed smile. 'Why don't we all discuss this later over dinner? You are staying to dinner, aren't you, David?' The normally practically assured woman looked less than certain for once.

David's expression gentled as he gazed at the other woman. 'Longer than that, if I'm welcome?' He looked a little shame-faced.

'Of course you are.' Penny blushed her pleasure. 'The kids will be overjoyed to see you.'

'I've missed them.' David's voice was husky with emotion now.

Jade was a little puzzled by the hesitant pleasure in Penny's face, at Simon's emotional smile as he looked on—but she was even more concerned about the thought of dinner tonight, not least because she had completely forgotten that she was supposed to be dining at the Kendricks' this evening! The first week she had arrived here Penny and Simon had invited her over to dinner on a Friday night, a practice that had continued, and as today was a Friday... She had no intention of meeting David Kendrick ever again, and certainly not over a cosy family dinner tonight!

'Maybe I should give dinner a miss for tonight?' she hastened to excuse herself. 'You all sound as if you have quite a lot of catching up to do, and so——'

'My dear, most of the talk will be about you, if I read my little brother correctly,' Simon drawled in an amused voice, blue eyes twinkling teasingly. 'So you might as well come along as arranged and avoid all that unnecessary ear-burning!'

It was her face that burnt now. Penny and Simon really were the nicest couple—she could believe that again now she knew Simon hadn't turned into a drunken lecher!—and she had greatly appreciated those weekly dinners with them in the past, but she really would rather not spend any more time in David Kendrick's company than she had to.

He seemed to sense her impending refusal, giving a wry smile. 'I really haven't "escaped" from anywhere—although I understand if at the moment you think perhaps I ought to have done!' he acknowledged ruefully. 'But if anyone opts out of dinner tonight it really should be me; I'm the unexpected guest.'

And, as he very well knew, a very welcome one!

Jade frowned her irritation at his deliberate manipulation of the circumstances; she would look very petty now if she still insisted on refusing the invitation.

'I'll be around at eight o'clock as usual,' she finally answered Simon, completely ignoring David Kendrick, hoping that the way that she swept from the tiny room was regal and didn't show how she really felt—like a frightened rabbit!

David Kendrick had had a very determined glint in his eye as she turned to leave, and *she* seemed to be the purpose he was determined on.

'And now I have to spend the whole evening in his company,' she wailed to Wellington as they still sat in front of the glowing fireplace, only to look down and find he had gone to sleep somewhere in the middle of her tale. 'A lot of help you are!' she muttered, getting up to leave the cosily warm lounge with long strides to enter her much cooler bedroom; the radiators that heated the tiny cottage were warmed by the coal fire, and as that had only been alight a short time...

It was only one of the things she had found strange to adjust to when she moved into the cottage, being what she had always considered a 'townie', with all the modern conveniences that conveyed; central heating had been taken for granted back in her flat in London. Having coal delivered, lighting the fire each day, *keeping* it alight, were all alien to her. She usually found that the cottage had just reached an acceptable temperature when it was time to go to bed, but then the fire would go out during the night and she would get up to a freezing cold bedroom! Still, the cottage did have its advantages, the major one being that the cottage was so pretty that you quickly forgot about the lack of heating and the dozen or so other little quirks it had. A thatched cottage, with all of its original beams still intact, was still the sort of home 'townies' dreamt about.

And, despite what she had heard about villages, the neighbours were all so friendly; unobtrusive, but helpful if they should be needed.

Not that Jade 'needed' them very often, preferring, apart from her inevitable involvement with school mothers, to keep herself to herself. The locals seemed to accept that being from London made her prefer it that way. Although she wasn't actually from London originally, what was left of her family—and that wasn't a great deal—still lived in the Yorkshire town she had grown up in. But she rarely returned there now.

Usually she looked forward to these Friday evening dinners as her only social outing of the week, a time when the three of them had mutually agreed not to discuss work but to simply enjoy each other's company. But tonight that was marred by the presence of *that* man.

David Kendrick. What was he really like under all that make-up and disguise? Simon's brown hair, which was thinning a little on top, was cut more for practicality than style; would his brother's be the same? Their eyes, she knew, were the same deep blue, just as their voices were very similar, but the rest of David Kendrick was an enigma. For all she knew, there might not have been any padding under the Father Christmas costume! Even as the slightly ridiculous idea came to mind, she knew, by the slenderness of his hands and the cotton pads in his mouth to make his cheeks look fatter, that David Kendrick had probably needed more padding than his brother to play the role.

He was probably handsome as the devil, and with a charm to match—and he had claimed he intended to marry her!

Marriage wasn't something she contemplated with anyone, let alone when suggested to her by a complete stranger who had made her seriously doubt his sanity by his strange behaviour!

Maybe he wouldn't be handsome, after all; maybe he had a permanent squint, or acne? There had to be something wrong with him—besides his tendency towards insanity—for him to still be single in the early to mid-thirties he must be to be Simon's 'younger' brother. Insanity certainly wouldn't exclude a reasonably eligible man of that age from the marriage market, not if some of the married couples she had observed were anything to go by!

Oh, well, she didn't have the time to speculate about him any more, had to get ready if she wasn't to be late for dinner. And within a few minutes of her arrival at the Kendricks' all her questions would be answered anyway. Hopefully David Kendrick would also have either sobered up or become sane again by then!

It was as she went to pull the curtains over her tiny bedroom window that she noticed the falling snow for the first time; no wonder Wellington had opted for a comfortable night in front of the fire instead of his usual round of girlfriends.

The snow couldn't have been falling very long, but already there was a white covering of it on her pathway, although only a light dusting of it on the garden itself. But the flakes were quite large, and if it continued to fall at this rate...

She only needed the lightest of excuses not to go to dinner tonight, and surely falling snow could be classed as a little more than that?

But, even as a sense of relief at being spared the ordeal washed over her, she saw the headlights of an approaching vehicle coming towards her driveway. Almost instantly she recognised the vehicle as the silver-coloured Range Rover Simon occasionally used to transport the children to and from school during bad weather; the Kendricks certainly weren't going to take any chances of her opting out of this evening's plans! Or maybe Simon had made the two-mile trip from his house to her cottage at his brother's request; from what she remembered of David Kendrick, she had a feeling he could just be persistent enough to do that.

'It's all right for you,' she muttered to Wellington as she passed him on her way to answer the knock on the door. 'You're assured of a nice, comfortable evening.' As she had expected, the cat just ignored her grumblings, too sleepy and warm to even twitch an ear at the sound of her voice.

Jade gave an impatient sigh, wrenching open the cottage door.

Outside, the snow falling on hair so dark it was almost black, was the most lethally attractive man she had ever seen...

The dark hair lightly brushed the collar of the black leather jacket that was zipped half-way up the powerful chest, a chest that tapered down to a narrow waist and muscular thighs beneath tailored black trousers. There could be no doubt about it, David Kendrick had needed plenty of padding beneath the Father Christmas costume, for the rounded waistline at least, although his shoulders looked wide enough to fill the suit without any help.

She knew it was him by his eyes, navy blue eyes that looked at her as if he were eating her up. And there wasn't a squint in sight!

Just as there wasn't a single mark on the devastatingly handsome face, the nose long and straight, high cheekbones, fuller lower lip that hinted at a passionate nature. As if she needed any hints after his behaviour earlier today! If Penny hadn't walked in on them in the store-cupboard when she had, she might have received conclusive proof of just how passionate he was.

But the sensuality was there in the pleased slant of his mouth, in the blue gaze that didn't leave her face for a moment, and the hard muscles of his body were full of male challenge.

His smile widened, revealing evenly white teeth; God, didn't this man have a single defect? Of course he did, she remembered with some relief, he was more than a little strange!

'Hello, I'm——'

'David Kendrick,' she finished abruptly, nodding. 'I know.'

'I wasn't sure you would recognise me without my disguise,' he drawled, his voice pleasantly deep without the cotton wool pads he had had stuffed into his cheeks earlier.

Oh, she had recognised him, all right, probably would have done so even without the help of his arrival in the Range Rover; she was never likely to forget the deep blue of his eyes, the only part of him that had really been recognisable beneath the Father Christmas disguise.

'Penny and Simon sent me over to get you in case the snow put you off coming,' he offered by way of explanation when she made no effort to continue the conversation.

Green eyes flared with resentment. She was pretty confident that the idea to come and collect her had been mainly David Kendrick's.

'All right,' he murmured indulgently, that enticing half-smile on his lips. '*I* had no intention of letting you cry off dinner tonight.'

Jade had to admire his honesty—even if it was what she had already known!

There were a lot of things about this man she could have admired if things had been different. But they weren't, and so she viewed him with the same wariness she did all strangers—more so, because he was even *stranger* than most!

Her gaze met his coolly. 'I would have telephoned if I hadn't intended coming,' she dismissed.

He grinned confidently. 'Now there's no reason
for you to have to do so. And don't worry about
being able to get back later tonight; the Range
Rover can easily get through any English snowfall.'

Giving the impression that this man had been in
places where the vehicle wouldn't have stood a
chance of doing that. Jade looked at him speculatively. Yes, he looked like a well-travelled and intelligent man, someone she would normally have
found fascinating to talk to. Normally. Unfortunately, the situation wasn't normal; how could it
be, when the man was so outrageous?

Her mouth tightened. 'Would you care to wait
in the living-room while I go and change?' Her tone
was distinctly distant.

He smiled, unperturbed by her offhand manner.
'I thought you would never ask,' he murmured as
he strolled past her into the tiny room behind,
pausing to look around him appreciatively at the
antique furniture and décor she had deliberately
chosen to complement the olde worlde character of
the cottage.

'Hello, boy.' He went down on his haunches to
tickle Wellington on his silkily soft tummy. 'At least
you have the right idea,' he continued ruefully, still
hunched down beside the cat.

Jade mentally acknowledged that a quiet evening
spent in front of the glowing fire certainly held more
appeal for her than one spent in this man's
company. As for Wellington, he was behaving like

a complete traitor; usually he ran away to hide when confronted by someone he wasn't familiar with, which was virtually everyone, but with David Kendrick he looked to be in ecstasies, an uncharacteristic look of total stupidity on his face as he still lay on his back, having his tummy stroked.

'I'll go and change,' she repeated stiltedly, turning abruptly to leave the room.

When David Kendrick stood up to turn towards her he was holding Wellington in his arms, still tickling him under the chin—and if Jade hadn't known better she would have sworn the silly feline was actually smiling. Damn it, he *was* smiling!

'Mind he doesn't scratch you,' she warned sharply. 'He has been known to do that without warning.'

Dark brows rose over mocking blue eyes. 'It's always the ones that look the friendliest that do that,' he said softly.

Jade felt the colour warm her cheeks at his obvious double meaning. 'It's a question of watching the eyes,' she snapped.

His mouth quirked. 'I'll try and remember that.'

'Do,' she bit out, trying not to hurry from the room but knowing she hadn't really succeeded; something about David Kendrick made her very nervous. Which was ridiculous. She was a teacher, for goodness' sake, a responsible adult in charge of seventeen pupils on a day-to-day basis—and heaven knew, children could be complex enough to deal with on occasion. And yet David Kendrick completely disconcerted her. Maybe it was the fact that he seemed to have come so close so quickly; usually she didn't allow the type of familiarity he had taken for granted from the first. Whatever the reason, and despite the dinner they would be sharing this evening in the company of Penny and Simon, she had no intention of allowing him to come any closer.

It seemed petty, not to mention childish, to choose her most unattractive outfit to wear for the evening ahead, but she really didn't have that big a selection in her wardrobe. Her only social occasions were spent at the Kendricks', and they didn't bother about 'dressing' for the evening. Unless tonight was going to be different because of the presence of David Kendrick... But no, while David's clothes had obviously been fashionable and of good quality, they had been casual clothes, not in the least formal. She would feel almost dowdy against him in her serviceable navy blue skirt and practical cream blouse. Men really shouldn't be allowed to be so perfect to look at that they were almost beautiful!

Remembering the remark he had made earlier about her hair, she pulled the auburn tresses back in so tight a bun that it made her eyes smart! The pressure eased as she loosened it a little, and with a rueful shrug she realised that now she *was* behaving childishly. She only removed her glasses briefly, so that she could apply a little blue shadow to her lids, before firmly placing the shield back on the bridge of her nose. They acted as a barrier against people like David Kendrick, and she had no intention of going anywhere without them, despite the accuracy of his mocking comment earlier today about them being unnecessary. Or *in spite* of it!

As she surveyed the final result of her ten-minute change of clothes she knew that she didn't look so very different from when she had started, but she felt comfortable like this, and certainly had no intention of trying to impress David Kendrick.

Her expression was one of challenge as he turned to look at her from contemplating the falling snow out of the window. 'Is it still snowing as heavily?' Her tone was defensively sharp as she waited for some critical comment about her relatively unchanged appearance.

'No,' he dismissed. 'You look beautiful,' he told her huskily.

Her cheeks coloured warmly at the unexpected compliment. 'We should leave now if we don't want to be late,' she bit out.

His mouth quirked. 'Something else I'll have to remember; you don't like compliments,' he explained self-derisively.

Jade pulled on her coat without asking his assistance, the expression in her eyes enough to warn him against offering.

'You're right about the eyes,' he murmured softly, laughter glinting in his own dark blue depths.

She shot him a reproving glare. 'If you've quite finished amusing yourself...?' She stood pointedly beside the front door.

David strode across the small living-room with soft footsteps, pausing just in front of Jade. 'I'm not laughing *at* you, Jade,' he murmured softly, perfectly serious now. 'It's just been years since I felt this damned happy, and I can't seem to stop myself smiling!'

She shot him a puzzled glance as he stood at her side while she locked the cottage door behind them, reminded once again that Penny and Simon had never mentioned he had a younger brother; there was obviously some mystery there, and now she couldn't help wondering if it weren't connected with David Kendrick's past unhappiness.

But who was she to question or speculate about another person's past? Anyone probing into her own past was likely to receive a very cutting reply.

She was deep in thought as they began the drive to Penny and Simon's house, aware of the questioning looks David Kendrick kept shooting in her direction, but doing her best not to acknowledge them.

She would get through tonight because she had already accepted Penny and Simon's invitation long before David Kendrick's arrival, but after that she was determined to stay away from the Kendrick family for the duration of David's visit.

'You remind me of someone, you know,' he suddenly said into the darkness, startling Jade out of the hypnotic dream she had fallen into as she watched the snow gently falling against the windscreen.

It was perhaps as well that he couldn't see how pale she had become in the darkness. No one had recognised her since she had come to this quiet little village, her role as a local teacher deflecting questions about her personal life to a certain degree. And now this man, a man who had done nothing but disturb and upset her from the first, claimed to know her.

'She gave me a black eye at our first meeting, too,' he continued musingly.

Jade had guiltily noticed that slight discoloration about his eye on his arrival, but had been too embarrassed—and angry!—about the whole incident to bring attention to it.

She gave an irritated frown now, still disturbed by his claim of recognising her. 'Who did?' she asked distractedly.

She didn't *want* to move on from this job until she had to; she loved the school and the pupils. And yet David Kendrick could leave her with no choice.

He gave her an indulgent smile before his attention returned to the road in front of them, that brief glance not seeming to have revealed the paleness of her cheeks to him. 'The lovely lady you remind me of,' he answered shruggingly.

Jade's frown deepened, and then her expression cleared with some relief as the significance of his words struck her. 'You have someone specific in mind?' she realised slowly.

'Oh, yes.' He grinned his satisfaction at having her undivided attention now. 'As I said, she slapped my face at our first meeting, too.' He shot her a triumphant smile. 'And a week later I married her!'

CHAPTER THREE

JADE gaped at him, couldn't do anything else in the circumstances. If he had married this other woman, then what—— God, he *was* deranged, and once this other woman had realised that she had obviously opted out of the situation. And who could blame her?

'All that proves,' she snapped waspishly, 'is that you're a consistently annoying man!'

He chuckled softly. 'Sara often thought so. But she always forgave me.' He quirked his brows questioningly. 'Are you going to do the same?'

She looked at him uncertainly.

He gave a rueful smile. 'You were right about my behaviour earlier—it was outrageous, and I am ashamed of myself.'

Jade sighed. 'That's something, at least,' she said tartly.

He nodded. 'Of course, it doesn't change the fact that I *do* want to marry you,' he told her lightly.

'Wouldn't Sara have something to say about that?' Her sarcasm was unmistakable.

'Sara's dead,' he explained softly. 'She has been for a number of years. And please don't apologise,' he drawled. 'It really was years ago.'

Jade's cheeks still burnt from the gaffe, burning anew at his mocking acknowledgement of it. How could she have even guessed that his wife had died, especially as she must have been relatively young? Oh, hell, she should have at least *thought* of the possibility. Now she really did feel as if she should apologise, which was exactly the disadvantage David Kendrick wanted to put her at, she felt sure. Not that his regret over his wife's death wasn't genuine, she felt certain it was; he was just mischievous enough to enjoy her discomfort, whatever the reason.

'That's how I knew the slap was a sign,' David Kendrick continued with satisfaction. 'Especially when the second one resulted in this.' He ran triumphant fingertips over the slight bruising at his eye.

Jade frowned, wishing the journey over so that at least Penny and Simon could act as a buffer between her and this strange man. 'A sign?' she repeated warily.

'That Sara knew and approved of the instantaneous attraction I felt towards you,' he nodded. 'That she understood the time had come for that "other door to open" in my life, that she even accepted you.'

Understood and accepted——? Dead women didn't give their husbands 'signs' like that! Besides, she didn't like the idea of possibly being instrumental in that 'sign'—it made her feel uncomfortable, to say the least. The very least!

'There's only one problem with that notion,' she bit out sharply. 'I have no wish to *be* in your life.'

He grimaced. 'After the stunt I pulled earlier by not instantly correcting you over the mistaken identity, I'm not surprised, but—'

'What *were* you doing playing Father Christmas instead of Simon?' Curiosity got the better of her.

'Surprising Penny,' he explained ruefully.

Remembering how pale the other woman had gone when she had instantly realised the man behind the Father Christmas suit wasn't her husband but his younger brother, she would say he had succeeded very well in achieving that!

He sighed, undeterred by Jade's silence. 'You see, we haven't seen each other for—a number of years. My fault, I'm afraid,' he admitted heavily. 'But when the two people you love most in the world remind you too painfully of the one person you ever loved more than them, the easiest—and probably the hardest, too!—thing to do is put them out of your life at the same time as you block out the pain of losing that special someone you loved.'

Jade felt as if she were being privileged with an insight into this man very few people were ever honoured with. And she, of all people, didn't want it, drew back from the intimacy of the confidence.

'That's understandable,' she dismissed stiffly, once again wishing the journey over.

David's mouth twisted. 'Fortunately Penny and Simon feel the same way about it that you do— otherwise my surprise could have ruined more than one Christmas.'

And instead only her own plans for the festive season seemed to have been affected. The

Kendricks had invited her to spend several pre-Christmas celebrations with them during the next few days, but with David Kendrick obviously now in on those invitations too... She would rather go back to her original plan of spending a quiet few weeks with Wellington than deliberately thrusting herself into this man's company.

'We all used to spend so much time together,' David murmured absently, obviously deeply lost in thought. 'Penny and Simon, Sara and me.' He gave a wistful sigh. 'Penny and Sara were more like sisters.'

'I was at college with Penny's younger sister,' Jade blurted out as a change of subject, knowing she hadn't quite succeeded when David smiled his satisfaction.

'Penny somehow seems to have a natural affinity with the women I'm going to marry,' he said with satisfaction.

'How many of us were there at the last count?' she felt stung into retorting.

David gave her a reproving look. 'Do I look like the sort of man who's had a string of wives?'

He *looked* like the sort of man who had never given marriage a thought, the perennial bachelor, in fact. But that could be because, by his own admission, his marriage to Sara had been so long ago.

Jade sighed. 'You look like the sort of man who has had a string of *women* in his life,' she taunted challengingly.

His expression became completely serious, those deep blue eyes looking almost black in the darkness.

'A few,' he admitted thoughtfully. 'Although not necessarily in the way you mean.' He smiled, as if he couldn't help himself. 'Ask me to introduce you to Dizzy and Christi some time. They are the only two women who have been in my life for some time.'

Dizzy and Christi? They didn't sound like the sort of women she would like to meet at all—or who would like to meet her either, for that matter!

'I don't think so, thank you,' she declined frostily.

'I just know you're all going to get along well together,' he said with certainty.

He was expecting a lot, thinking she wanted to be introduced to his harem. Although maybe she was supposed to feel herself privileged; after all, he had offered *her* marriage!

'I doubt the opportunity will ever arise for us to "get along" or otherwise,' she told him drily.

'They're both good friends of mine,' he frowned.

'Exactly,' she said with saccharine sweetness.

God, was that really her sounding so condescending? She wasn't usually bitchy like this, but the fact that David Kendrick just wouldn't accept her lack of interest in him—or his friends!—seemed to have turned her into a shrew.

'What work do you do, Mr Kendrick?' she quickly changed the subject.

'David,' he instantly insisted, as Jade had known that he would. After all, they could hardly go on calling each other 'Mr Kendrick' and 'Miss Mellors' all evening. Penny and Simon might be decidedly uncomfortable about that, to say the least!

'Jade,' she returned distantly.

'I heard that earlier,' he said warmly. 'Looking at your eyes, it isn't difficult to understand why.'

'The colour of my eyes is purely coincidental,' she dismissed flatly. 'They were the usual blue when I was born, and didn't start to turn green until I was about three months old. The reason I was called Jade was because my father collected it. And I suppose at the time I was born he considered me as precious as his collection. But we were discussing you,' she reminded him sharply, regretting her lapse in revealing even that much about herself. Had any of the bitterness she felt at no longer being thought worthy of that place by her father shown in her voice or manner? David didn't seem unduly interested in the comment—thank God!

'The clear colour of your eyes is definitely the most beautiful thing I've ever seen,' David firmly corrected her first statement. 'It isn't in the least coincidental,' he chided her on the use of the term.

'You were going to tell me what work you do,' she prompted distantly, making no effort to hide her displeasure at the compliment. Even if it did sound completely genuine. *Especially* as it sounded completely genuine!

David shrugged, as if he considered the subject of his occupation well down his list of priorities. It was also obvious what—or rather, who—was at the top of it. 'I publish books,' he dismissed uninterestedly.

Her brows rose with mocking censure. 'Really?' she drawled derisively.

'Not those sort of books,' David chuckled with emphasis as he correctly read the thought that was going through her mind. 'Ever heard of Empire Publishing?' He quirked mocking brows, as if her condescension greatly amused him.

As well it might! Good lord, it was like asking an Englishman if he had ever heard of cricket, the Dutch tulips, the Americans hamburgers, the Germans——Empire Publishing company was constantly on the top of the best-seller list with its numerous popular authors. And its entrepreneur owner was reputedly responsible for personally recognising the majority of those talents. How could she have possibly known Simon's younger brother was *that* David Kendrick?

'Claudia Laurence is one of my favourite authors,' she admitted in an uncomfortable voice, aware that once again she was at a disadvantage.

Her admission only made David chuckle even more. 'Remind me to introduce her to you some time.' He made an effort to contain his humour, only partially succeeding as he still grinned widely.

Jade wondered disgruntledly what was so funny about having admitted she admired his most talented author. 'I thought Miss Laurence liked her privacy.' Her tone was sharp. Really, his habit of finding her a source of amusement was beginning to rankle! No one had ever found her *this* funny before, that she knew of.

'She does,' David nodded, that devilish gleam of laughter still in his eyes. 'But I think she might make

the exception for a close friend of mine,' he added
with certainty.

'Something which I most definitely am not,' Jade
snapped, noticing with relief that their slow journey
was almost over, the lights of the Kendrick house
coming into sight.

'You're going to be,' he told her confidently as
he turned the vehicle into the driveway.

She had learnt a distaste of arrogant men, had
found that arrogance was usually accompanied by
selfishness, and maybe if David Kendrick had
sounded in the least arrogant as he made the
statement her wariness of him would have been well
justified, but instead he just sounded totally convinced he was right, which wasn't the same thing
at all!

Jade had her door open and had stepped down
from the Range Rover before David had a chance
to get around to her, once again finding herself on
the receiving end of his amused glance as he easily
guessed the reason for her haste.

'I always feel sorry for those chaps this time of
year.' He motioned in the direction of a passing
police car as he took a firm hold of her arm,
walking towards the house. 'It must be hell keeping
an eye open for all those after-work-party drunks
that suddenly take to the roads.' He shook his head.
'I think they must have thought I was one for a
while; they were on my tail almost as soon as we
left your cottage.'

Jade's alarmed gaze followed the departure of
the police car as it slowly cruised along out of sight,

given no real chance to question the incident as Penny opened the door to greet them before taking them into the warm comfort that was the Kendricks' home.

Situated in the school grounds, the house had once been the original cottage hospital that existed on the site, and Penny had worked wonders transforming what could have been a barn of a place into a warmly welcoming refuge for all the family and their friends. Lavishly festooned with Christmas decorations, most made for them by the pupils, at the moment it had extra appeal, everywhere bright and glittery, but most of all, warm.

'I hope this clown has apologised for his behaviour earlier,' Penny lightly scolded as she took their damp coats—although it was obvious by her open affection as she gazed at David that she would forgive this man anything—and probably had during the last few hours.

'Profusely,' he grinned, more handsome than ever in the intimacy of the hallway.

'He has—explained the situation,' Jade acknowledged more formally, inwardly wishing she didn't sound so stiff and prim. But this man put her on the defensive, damn him.

'Although she doesn't accept that the slap—and this,' he indicated the discoloration at his eye, 'was a sign, either.' He shook his head sadly.

'Let's not start *that* again.' Penny very firmly pushed him towards the living-room. 'Go and help Simon pour out the drinks,' she instructed firmly, her usual air of authority obviously firmly back in place.

'Women's talk?' David teased softly.

'An attempt on my part to convince Jade you really don't need locking away!' Penny retorted. 'You see,' she pounced as Jade gave a rueful smile. 'She's obviously deeply sceptical that I can convince her of any such thing!' she told him disgustedly.

'It doesn't make any difference whether Jade thinks I'm insane or not,' David announced confidently. 'I still intend to marry her.'

'You would need my consent for that,' Jade snapped, her tone telling him that was something he would never get—unless *she* was insane!

'I'm not going to take no for an——'

'Will you go away, before Jade runs screaming into the night?' Penny told him exasperatedly. 'We don't see you for more years than I care to mention, and the first thing you do when we do see you is try to scare off one of our best teachers!'

'She is wonderful with children,' David acknowledged warmly, as if the fact pleased him enormously.

'Oh, God, don't tell me you have half a dozen of them that need a mother,' Jade groaned.

'Not yet,' he drawled. 'But we'll start work on it as soon as we're married.'

Jade felt completely drained as, having made yet another outrageous statement, he finally took Penny's advice and disappeared into the living-room in search of his brother.

'I know,' Penny said with a sigh as she met Jade's pained glance. 'He exhausts me as badly. I was always grateful that it was Simon I fell in love with and not David; who needs a whirlwind constantly upsetting their life?'

Who indeed? Certainly not Jade. She liked her life to be quiet, peaceful, and most of all without problems, either in fact or looming on the horizon.

Which reminded her very forcefully of the police car David had said followed them from her cottage. Had the police really been following them because they suspected David might have been one of those people who over-indulged in Christmas cheer, or had it been for another reason entirely?

She chided herself for being over-imaginative. David Kendrick's behaviour had upset her more than she realised; there could be no other reason than a routine observation for the policemen's interest in them.

'If the way David is acting is really bothering you, I can always try having another private word with him.' Penny was frowningly watching the fleeting expressions that crossed Jade's face, half right in her surmise that David *was* bothering her.

Jade shook off her distracted thoughts with effort. 'Would it do any good?' she smiled, the other woman's earlier effort having obviously failed.

Penny grimaced. 'I doubt it, the mood David is in, but I could try.'

'Don't bother.' She shook her head. 'I'm sure I can cope with the situation.'

'I'm sure you can,' Penny chuckled. 'Which is why I told Simon we should stay out of it. And if you don't manage to handle it—well, I think it might be rather nice to have you for a sister-in-law!' She softly laughed her enjoyment of the stunned expression on Jade's face before sweeping into the living-room ahead of her, having successfully made her point that David Kendrick could be like an express train if he chose—just as unstoppable.

Jade felt herself the sole attraction for a pair of dark blue eyes as she followed Penny into the room at a more leisurely pace, feeling her confidence slip a couple of notches at the determined glint in those dark depths. She had no plans to marry—ever—and she certainly wasn't going to be bullied into it!

'You braved it, after all,' Simon drawled from his standing position across the room, a blazing fire just to the left of him, chuckling softly as Jade's startled gaze was turned towards him. 'I meant the weather,' he softly explained.

Her cheeks burnt at the assumption she had made, and then she saw the devilish gleam in Simon's eyes that exactly matched that of his brother. He was finding all of this very amusing! And why shouldn't he? He wasn't on the receiving end of the lunacy.

'Do leave her alone, Simon,' Penny chided. 'It's enough that she has one idiot making her life miserable.'

'Hm,' he acknowledged, giving Jade an apologetic look. 'Just let me know if David gets too much for you,' he advised. 'I always could beat him in a fair fight.'

Dark brows rose over confident blue eyes. 'Who says I intend to fight fair this time? You know the saying...'

The affection between the two men was tangible, and Jade had a feeling that if it really came down to it Simon was perfectly capable of aiding his brother in his claim to marrying her! Two Kendrick men on the same side would probably defeat anyone.

Which was why she took the earliest opportunity—while she and Penny were washing up after the meal and the two men were indulging in a friendly game of billiards—to make her excuses to Penny for the arrangements they had made for her to spend time with them during the holiday period.

Penny looked deeply disappointed, a frown over her dark brown eyes. 'I'd been looking forward to your company,' she sighed.

Jade instantly felt ungrateful, and more than a little selfish; after all, the Kendricks had opened their hearts and their home to her.

'And Cathy has promised to try and get down for a day or two because you're here,' Penny chided.

That wasn't strictly true, although she knew Cathy was making a special effort to try and get time off from her exacting job as personal assistant to a man who didn't seem to acknowledge that holidays existed. And if she did manage to get away for a couple of days it would have been nice to see her friend...

But David Kendrick was here, too.

And that said it all . . .

'Besides,' Penny pressed at her continued silence, 'all my plans have been made with a certain number in mind.'

'David's here now,' Jade pointed out drily.

'That just means I have to come up with another woman for the dinner parties, not lose one of the ones I've already got!' Penny reminded exasperatedly.

Jade gave a sigh. It seemed there was no way she could get out of the plans already made without insulting the couple who had been so kind to her. Penny was probably wondering what she was doing running scared just because David was chasing her so hard; after all, there couldn't be that many women who would actually want to run! David Kendrick was everything that was eligible: handsome, fun, charming, rich. Even that tendency he had to be rather intense wouldn't diminish some women's interest, and now that she knew about his first wife she could better understand the conclusions he had drawn about the slaps she had given him. Although that certainly didn't mean she believed in that nonsense! She had slapped him because he'd been acting so strangely, not because she had been inspired to do so by a dead woman. Although she couldn't help but feel curious as to why Sara had administered *her* slap all those years ago . . .

No doubt Penny knew, and would probably enjoy telling her, but she didn't want to seem in the least interested in David Kendrick or his past.

'If it's going to upset things for you...' she reluctantly gave in.

'It is,' the other woman instantly accepted, her expression brightening. 'And if Cathy does turn up, maybe I won't have to find a partner for David for long.'

Jade had no doubts that David could find his own partner, all too easily; she was also certain he would do no such thing when he was so intent on capturing her.

'That's all settled, then,' Penny said briskly as she tidied away the washed and dried crockery. 'I have to admit, I thought I was going to have more trouble convincing you than that,' she confided cheekily.

She gave the other woman a reproving look, mentally berating herself for being so gullible.

'Hey, Simon and I really aren't going to abandon you to his clutches,' Penny chided at her frowning expression.

As David insisted on being the one to drive her back home a short time later, Jade knew the other couple weren't going to be given much choice. Beneath the charm and fun was a will of iron, apparently!

'Cheer up,' he advised lightly as he did up his seat-belt beside her. 'I'm not about to ravish you as soon as we reach your cottage.'

Jade gave him a dismissive glance, considering the remark not even worthy of a reply. Of course he wasn't about to ravish her, he was a man in his mid-thirties, hardly still in the juvenile stage!

'Which isn't to say,' he added softly as he manoeuvred the Range Rover out on to the road, 'that I'm not going to try to steal a kiss or two.' His eyes gleamed with intent.

She felt her cheeks pale, her lips suddenly stiff. 'No one takes anything from me that I don't wish to give,' she bit out harshly. Not any more, no one did that to Jade any more!

David shot her a questioning glance. 'That was said with rather a lot of feeling?'

'And shouldn't it have been?' she returned defensively. 'What right do you have to try to take something I don't want to give?' Her eyes flashed deeply green.

'I don't take, Jade,' he told her gently, the hand nearest to her reaching out to clasp hers as it rested against her thigh, his hand tightening fractionally as he felt her stiffen, before slowly releasing her. 'Sara didn't slap me because she was physically afraid of me,' he explained softly.

'Sara?' Jade gave him a sharp look. 'What does your wife have to do with this?' Surely that was the last subject they should be discussing in the circumstances?

'I thought maybe you had imagined I had tried to "ravish" her on our first meeting, and that was the reason for your wariness... Obviously I was wrong,' he murmured thoughtfully. 'Would you like to hear why Sara *did* slap me?' he enquired lightly, just as if the last few moments of tension hadn't happened.

Jade was disconcerted, realising that perhaps she was supposed to be, but too relieved by the change of subject to question it. 'I'd love to know what Sara could possibly have found so irritating about you that she resorted to physical violence on your first meeting.' Her tone implied she couldn't imagine a man who had deserved the slap more.

David chuckled softly. 'She thought I was having an affair with her mother.'

Jade gasped; she couldn't help it. Whatever she had been expecting, it certainly hadn't been that!

'It wasn't true, of course,' he added drily.

She raised auburn brows, more in control again now. 'It wasn't?' she mocked.

He gave a rueful smile. 'I know you would love to think it was, but unfortunately it wasn't. Judy was, and is, a lovely woman,' he derided at her questioning look, chuckling as she looked suitably taken aback. 'She was also one of the first authors I signed for Empire: Judy Maxwell.'

Jade knew the author well, another of her favourites, specialising in those big blockbuster sagas that were always so popular.

'We had been having a series of meetings about a manuscript she had submitted to me, and because Judy wanted to surprise her family with her "success", she hadn't told any of them she had sent the manuscript off to a publisher, let alone that we actually wanted to talk to her about it. The first I knew that Sara had found out about the meetings and drawn the wrong conclusion was when this black-haired vixen came into my office and accused me of seducing her mother, just as she punched me in the eye. She was nineteen at the time, full of idealism, and seducing her mother, even though Judy had been a widow for over five years, just wasn't on,' he remembered fondly.

The affection and love he had felt for his wife was all there in his voice, and once again Jade had the feeling of intruding on something that was intensely private.

'But the two of you did marry a week later,' she prompted abruptly, the snow having stopped falling some time during the course of the evening, the heavy vehicle finding the journey easily manageable. Thank goodness!

He nodded. 'With me still sporting the black eye she had given me,' he smiled. 'Once Judy and I had calmed Sara down enough to listen, we explained the true situation to her. And once she had calmed down I realised she was even more beautiful then than she had been when she was angry; I lost no time in inviting her out to dinner. Within a few days we were inseparable, and when we decided to marry there was no doubt in either of our minds that we were making the right decision.'

But Sara had died, and from the sound of it that emotional side of this man's life had died along with her. Until now. She should feel honoured that David considered *her* worthy enough to take his beloved Sara's place, but she only felt panic.

'Judy was a terrific mother-in-law,' David recalled fondly. 'We're still very good friends. And we always get together on the anniversary of Sara's death.' There was naked pain in his voice as he spoke of it.

'She must have been very young,' Jade's voice was gruff.

'Only twenty,' he nodded grimly. 'We had only been married a year. She had leukaemia, we found out soon after our wedding. Nineteen years old and already condemned to die,' he said harshly. 'We put a lifetime of loving into that year, fulfilled all her dreams. Except one. A child,' he explained softly as he sensed Jade's questioning look, staring ahead into the darkness. 'She would have been a wonderful mother; she loved children as much as you do.'

Jade felt a familiar jolt as she realised that she was now the object of this man's emotions. And it sounded as if, when he loved, he loved long and deeply. God, she didn't want to see him hurt again after what he had just told her, but he had to be made to see that he had misplaced his affection, that she was totally unsuitable.

'I love teaching children,' she corrected. 'I've never envisaged having any of my own,' she lied, knowing that that particular dream had been buried some time ago, along with several others she had cherished.

'I won't push for that if it's something you feel strongly about,' David shrugged. 'It might have been nice to have a little girl with your auburn hair and jade-coloured eyes,' he added wistfully. 'But it isn't something I'm going to insist upon.'

He made her feel so helpless, with his certainty that there was a future for them, with or without children! How could you get through to a man who simply wouldn't listen?

He drew the Range Rover to a halt in her small driveway, turning in his seat to look at her after turning on the overhead light. 'I'll pick you up about eleven o'clock in the morning, shall I? Or do you prefer to sleep later than that?' He quirked dark brows.

'I would *prefer* not to be disturbed at all in the morning,' she told him frostily.

'OK,' he shrugged without rancour. 'I'll come over in the afternoon.'

'David——'

'I noticed you didn't have a tree at the cottage,' he cut in softly. 'I thought we could go and choose one together.'

The fact that he had noticed the lack of decorations at the cottage shouldn't have come as a surprise to her; he seemed to take note of everything about him, with little effort. The fact that he felt he had some right to rectify matters rankled.

He gave a pained grimace. 'I can see I've stepped on your toes again.'

Jade's cheeks became warm. 'It isn't that, I just wasn't going to bother with a tree this year. I shall be there so little, you see.' She was babbling, making excuses and explaining herself over something that was really none of this man's business. 'I thought I might spend more time picking it up after Wellington decided to play on it than I would looking at it,' she announced defensively.

'The cat?' he guessed correctly. 'He looked as if his interests lie in quite another direction,' he derided.

'The pine needles might damage his pads,' she insisted stubbornly.

'Then we'll buy one of those plastic ones that are supposed to be so realistic,' he suggested, undeterred.

Christmas trees with pine needles that her mother good-naturedly complained shed all over her carpet and constantly needed vacuuming up reminded her too vividly of Christmases spent at home with her family, of the warmth and happiness that had existed there. All of those things denied to her now.

'If I had wanted a tree, I would have bought one,' she snapped coldly, pushing open the door at her side. 'Thank you for bringing me home, Mr Kendrick. No doubt I will be seeing you again shortly.' She stood outside in the snow now.

'I'll walk you to the door.' David made a move to get out of the Range Rover.

'No need,' Jade told him shortly. 'There's no reason for both of us to get cold.'

He relaxed back in his seat. 'You can't keep running for ever, Jade,' he warned her softly.

'Running?' she echoed in a strangulated voice. 'What on earth do you mean?' Her hands were clenched at her sides.

'Running from me,' he said slowly, giving her a considering look. 'At least, that's what I *think* I meant,' he added with deep puzzlement, intrigued by her reaction.

Jade's eyes blazed. 'I'm not running from anyone or anything,' she grated harshly. 'Once again, thank you for the lift home.' She slammed the door behind her, not looking back as she trudged over to the cottage door, turning the key in the lock to close the door firmly behind her just as she heard the Range Rover engine leap back into life at the switch of the key.

She leant back against the closed cottage door, visibly shaken. For a moment, a very brief moment, she had imagined that somehow David Kendrick had guessed that the only man she had ever fallen in love with had stolen more than her heart, that he had taken so much more from her than that . . .

CHAPTER FOUR

THE thudding noise was soft, but irritating. Jade moved protestingly beneath the soft down of her quilt, the light behind her closed lids telling her it was morning, but the lethargy of her body also telling her it wasn't far enough into the morning for her to have to get out of bed yet. Besides, it was a Saturday.

The soft thudding continued, gently, but persistently.

'Go away, Wellington.' She dragged an arm from beneath the warmth, braving the chill air she knew would meet her outside of it, waving the cat away from whatever he was doing that was so annoying.

The soft thudding continued, gently, but persistently.

'If you want breakfast this morning, cat, I would advise you to stop that now,' she growled frustratedly.

The soft thudding noise came again—just about the same time she realised that the extra warmth on her feet was the still sleeping body of the innocent cat.

Jade gave a weary sigh, so tired she didn't *want* to wake up yet. It had been a restless night, memories she would rather not have relived flooding her mind until she had no choice but to face them. Sleep had been a long time coming after that.

And now that thudding, that out-of-tune-with-her-usual-morning-sounds noise persisted in disturbing her when she would rather have turned over and gone back to sleep for several hours.

But she knew she couldn't do that, that she would have to get up and investigate the sound, especially as they had had the first snowfall last night since she moved in here. One of the roofs could be leaking, or—— Suddenly sleep was the farthest thing from her mind; throwing back the duvet, her body immediately chilled as she quiveringly pulled on the thick robe she had found so helpful in recent weeks.

As she sat on the side of the bed she realised that the thudding noise was coming from the curtained window. The snow was melting already? There would be a lot of disappointed children this morning if that were the case.

She winced as she slightly parted the curtains and the white light from the blanket of snow that covered the ground instantly hit her.

It took her a few seconds to focus in the bright light of this winter morning, but when she did it was to realise there was a large mound of snow sliding down the window. Just as she realised that, a missile struck the window in front of her, causing her to pull back in alarm. And then she recognised it was only a snowball. But the snowball had to have been thrown by someone...

She instantly ruled out one of the village children, knowing even before she tentatively looked down into her tiny front garden who the culprit was.

David Kendrick grinned up at her cheekily, looking disgustingly healthy and robust in the early morning light, the cold air having added a glow to his hard cheeks.

Jade dropped the curtains back into place as if they had burnt her, anger ripping through her as she turned back into the bedroom.

'I should have known,' she muttered as she threw open her wardrobe door to pull out a pair of denims and a thick green jumper. 'I don't know what possessed me to blame you, Wellington,' she furiously apologised as she dragged the clothes on. 'You're the only male I *can* rely on not to let me down or annoy me!' She slammed the wardrobe door on her way out of the room, her feet in the knee-length boots making a clattering noise on the stairs as she ran down them.

David had just gathered up enough snow to make another missile as she threw the door open, his eyes full of devilment as he spied her in the doorway.

'Don't you dare,' she fumed warningly.

The glove-covered hand that held the snow slowly lowered, the black leather jacket worn over a dark blue jumper and denims today, his hair lightly ruffled by the gentle breeze, adding to his rakish attraction.

The last thing Jade wanted at this moment was to be reminded of his devilish charm!

He dusted the snow from his hands. 'No wonder the children listen when you talk,' he said ruefully.

'Well, if you will persist in acting like a child...' she returned waspishly. 'Do you realise what time of morning it is?' A quick glance at the clock on her mantel on her way to the front door had told her it was only just after eight o'clock.

'The best time of day for a snowball fight,' he told her disarmingly.

Jade was taken aback by the endearingly made statement. A snowball fight...!

'OK.' David held his hands up defensively, looking more boyish than ever. 'The truth of the matter is I've hardly slept all night for thinking of you, and I couldn't wait any longer to see if you really did exist or if I could possibly have dreamt you. You can't imagine the relief I felt when you pulled back the curtains a few minutes ago. And don't worry, I forgive you for deceiving me.'

Jade was totally disconcerted by his candid admissions, although she stiffened warily at the last. 'Deceiving you?' she echoed softly.

He nodded, that grin back in place. 'Your hair is gloriously silky when it's loose about your shoulders like that, and you certainly don't need your glasses.'

Her cheeks felt hot as she realised she had been in such a hurry to get down here and give him a verbal dressing-down that she hadn't even brushed her hair this morning, let alone confined it in its usual style, and her glasses still sat on the bedside cabinet...

Bending, she scooped up a handful of the icy snow. 'You're right about the latter,' she accepted at the same moment she drew back her arm and took aim with the snowball. It landed smack in the middle of his chest. 'I can certainly see well enough to hit large objects!' She faced him challengingly.

'Large objects——!' he repeated with a low whistle between his teeth. 'That's fighting talk, Miss Mellors,' he warned silkily as he bent to retaliate.

It was ridiculous—eight o'clock in the morning and she was having a snowball fight with a man who yesterday had given every impression of being disturbed. In fact he hadn't done a single thing to change that impression; waking her up in this way certainly didn't qualify!

After several minutes of exuberant snowball-throwing, the majority of them reaching their mark, they were both glowingly warm—on the inside, at least. On the outside it was a different story, their clothes damp and uncomfortable, Jade's hair no longer 'gloriously silky' but hanging in wet tendrils about her face, and as for her hands—— She hadn't even had the benefit of gloves.

'Time to go inside and get warm, I think,' David recognised as he saw her involuntary shiver.

'No.' She shook her head ruefully.

He frowned. 'That wasn't an improper suggestion.' His frown deepened. 'Why is it I find myself sounding like some Victorian suitor whenever I'm around you?' he said self-derisively.

'I have no idea,' she snapped, not even looking at him as she brushed the snow from her clothing.

'And the reason I said no was because it won't be much warmer inside; I haven't had a chance to light the fire yet,' she explained drily. 'It had nothing to do with keeping you out of my home.'

'In that case, I'll light the fire while you cook breakfast.'

Breakfast? She had no intention of cooking breakfast for him, this morning or any other morning. But she was already too late to stop him going into the cottage, she realised as he disappeared inside.

By the time she entered he was already shovelling out the dead ashes, laying the fire once he had completed that task. And doing it very professionally, too.

'That isn't the first time you've done that,' she admired grudgingly.

He glanced across the room at her, that grin once again in evidence. 'I don't live in an apartment in town, Jade,' he told her softly. 'I live in a house in Berkshire which can only be called rustic, and I enjoy lighting a fire for myself when I come in from work on long winter evenings. And no, Sara didn't live there with me,' he added gently, even as the vision of the couple sitting together in front of the glowing fire sprang into Jade's mind.

She frowned her consternation. 'I wish you would stop doing that,' she bit out resentfully.

'Reading your mind?' he sat back on his haunches. 'I think it's a measure of our instant rapport,' he shrugged.

'We don't have——'

'I bet you have eggs and bacon in your fridge just waiting to be cooked for breakfast,' he lightly interrupted her protest.

'That isn't so unusual,' she scoffed.

'Mushrooms, too?' he mocked.

Her cheeks burnt fiery red. 'What on earth makes you think that?' she said defensively.

'You had a second helping of them at dinner last night,' he shrugged.

'So did you,' she instantly accused him.

'Exactly,' he drawled, his brows raised.

Jade drew in a deep breath, letting it out again in a deep sigh. 'OK, so we both like mushrooms,' she admitted defeatedly.

'And we can have some with our bacon and eggs?' he requested wistfully.

A grown man, especially one as devastatingly attractive as this one, shouldn't also have the power to have the appeal of a little boy; it wasn't fair to the female population! And it was galling to think that even she, someone who had been totally disillusioned about men, should be affected by that appeal.

'The food was for my lunch,' she told him waspishly. 'I don't usually eat breakfast.'

'Indulge me,' he encouraged huskily.

She sighed again. 'I have the feeling people have been indulging you since you were in your cradle,' she said disgustedly, already knowing she was going to be another one who did exactly that—as far as the breakfast went, anyway! She defended her actions by telling herself she was hungry and might as well feed him as she was going to cook anyway.

She didn't wait for David's reply, turning to go into the kitchen, leaving him to earn his meal by lighting the fire.

It wasn't until she had the bacon and mushrooms sizzling under the grill and the eggs cooking on the stove that she questioned what her neighbours were going to think about the Range Rover parked in her driveway when they got out of their beds. It would look as if the vehicle had been there all night! After months of living quietly, slowly melding into the community, of remaining completely apart from any gossip that might be circulating, she was probably going to give them the tastiest titbit they had had for months.

'Why so pensive?'

She hadn't realised David had entered the tiny kitchen, but she turned at the sound of his voice, grimacing her distress. 'The locals are going to be full of speculation about the Range Rover being outside the cottage,' she sighed heavily.

'I won't ask if that bothers you,' David said gently. 'Because it obviously does. But with the aid of our much-respected headmaster's wife I'm sure we can come up with a perfectly feasible excuse for my being here this time of the morning.'

'You must think I'm being ridiculous——'

'Nothing of the sort,' he cut in with brisk assurance. 'I should be one of the first to realise how these misunderstandings are made,' he added ruefully.

Of course, he had met his beloved Sara through just such a misunderstanding!

'Don't look on this as another of those "signs",' Jade warned hastily. 'This is just me being overly cautious.' And with good reason; the last thing she needed was speculative gossip about her.

'Let's eat before the food gets cold,' he suggested gently, his gaze warm.

She still looked hesitant. 'As long as you don't think that I——'

'I *think* that Penny can inform everyone—before they ask—that she was the one that was concerned about your welfare out here on your own, after the snowfall last night, and sent me over to check up on you. Early,' he added with emphasis.

'*Very* early,' she grimaced as they sat side by side at the breakfast bar, which was all the seating arrangement for eating the tiny cottage allowed.

'Right,' he nodded, liberally buttering his toast. 'And while I'm on the subject of your living "out here",' he frowned, 'aren't you a little too much out on your own for safety?'

The fact that the cottage was situated on its own was one of the things she had found hardest to adapt to when she had first moved here, but now she liked the relative solitude its location provided. 'The nearest neighbour is only a couple of hundred yards away,' she answered chidingly.

'What if you should fall down and hurt yourself?' David's frown deepened as if the thought greatly disturbed him.

'I'm sure I could manage to crawl to the telephone somehow and call for help,' she drawled mockingly.

He gave her a censorious look. 'But what if you got trapped somewhere——'

'Like the coal cellar?' she taunted, at his melodrama.

'Exactly,' he pounced, very agitated now as his imagination worked overtime.

Jade shook her head, calmly forking up some bacon and a mushroom. 'I don't have one,' she informed him lightly before popping the food into her mouth, having worked up quite an appetite during their snowball fight.

David didn't look convinced. 'You could accidentally lock yourself in somewhere——'

'The loo, for example,' she nodded.

'Yes. You——'

'I don't have a lock on the loo door,' she sighed, the conversation beginning to irritate her now. 'Besides, there's a window,' she added firmly, determinedly taking another mouthful of her breakfast.

Dark brows rose. 'Big enough for you to climb out of?'

'Just about,' she nodded after some consideration. 'But not for you to climb in!' she warned.

He gave her a reproachful look. 'Do I look the cat-burglar type?'

'Wellington wouldn't let you steal him even if you were,' she returned pertly, trying to introduce levity into the conversation, something he seemed determined she wouldn't do!

'Very funny!' he grimaced, acknowledging her mockery.

'Talking of Wellington...' she mused as the cat strolled into the kitchen for his breakfast now that he had decided he had had enough sleep for the night. Jade got up to mix his food. 'He's all the protection I need; I'm sure he would run for help if I needed it,' she drawled before once again sitting down at the breakfast bar beside David.

'I'm glad you find it amusing——'

'That's the whole point. I don't,' she cut in with irritable impatience. 'I don't need anyone fussing around me.'

'I'm not——'

'Your food's getting cold,' she snapped with finality, no longer enjoying the meal herself. She had spent the last year distancing herself from people, and didn't intend being trapped into a relationship now, even if David Kendrick was one of the nicest men she had ever met.

Nice. Not the dull, uninteresting sort of nice that became boring after a while; he was too unpredictable ever to be that! But he was a truly nice man who cared about others, was concerned for and about them. Cared and was concerned about *her*.

Which was all the more reason for her not to become involved with him, in any way.

'Something else for me to remember about you,' he drawled as he finally picked up his own knife and fork in preparation for eating. 'You don't like to feel protected.'

She gave him a frosty look. 'Protection is one thing; it's when it curtails your personal freedom that it becomes intrusive.' She was being too harsh, and she knew it, feeling almost guilty as he gave a disappointed shrug before starting to eat his breakfast.

Jade's own appetite had deserted her. God, how she wished she dare allow herself the luxury of feeling protected, cosseted and loved. But to do that she would have to allow her defences to drop, and it had been a long and painful process building them up in the first place! Even the slight lapse she had made a few moments ago as she'd tried to banter him out of his concern for her had been a lowering of her defences she dared not repeat. David might begin to think she actually liked him. And that would never do.

She silently dismissed his compliments and thanks for the meal with a shrug of her shoulders, hurriedly clearing away, anxious now to cut his visit short.

David watched her with unruffled amusement, leaning back against one of the kitchen units as she tidied away the crockery he had just finished wiping. Jade's movements became more and more agitated under his steadily watchful gaze.

'Finished?' he enquired casually when Jade could find nothing else to put away.

'In here,' she accepted stiffly. 'But I usually go into town to do my shopping on a Saturday.'

He straightened, taking the keys to the Range Rover out of his denims pocket. 'Then what are we waiting for?'

Her brows rose at his intention of accompanying her. 'That wasn't an invitation.'

'Mine was,' he returned easily. 'How else are you going to get into town?'

'In my car, of——' She broke off with a pained groan. Faithful as Cleo was—she had had the Mini six years now without any serious problems with it—she very much doubted the little car would be able to travel in the couple of inches of snow that still covered the roads in this area. If only she had remembered that damned snow before she had mentioned going shopping! 'I can always leave the shopping until another day now that school has finished for the Christmas holidays,' she dismissed with bravado.

'No need,' David said pleasantly, a determined glint in his eyes. 'Not when I'm conveniently here to take you. Besides,' he added before she could protest again, 'who's to say the snow will clear in time for you to go "another day"?'

He was right, of course, and she couldn't go indefinitely without stocking up on food, the lack of storage space at the cottage meaning she never had too much in at one time. And, reliable as Cleo was, she couldn't expect the tiny car to contend with the roads in this weather. 'Then I accept your kind invitation,' she told him stiltedly—both of them knowing she didn't really have a choice. 'I'll just go upstairs and get my coat.'

Damn, damn, *damn*! Going out to do her weekly shopping had seemed like the ideal way to escape any more of David's company today without having to be rude and actually ask him to go. Now she had unwittingly put herself in the position of being with him for a couple of hours more at least.

It wasn't until she got into her bedroom and accidentally caught sight of her reflection in the small dressing-table mirror that she realised her hair was still a silkily loose auburn cloud about her shoulders and her glasses were still conspicuously absent from the bridge of her nose.

Futile as it seemed, she went through the daily ritual of securing her hair and putting on the shield of her dark-rimmed glasses. She would have felt more businesslike in one of her plain skirts and blouses, but the thought of how cold it was outside was enough to keep her in the denims and jumper. She had already spent the last two hours in David's company dressed like this; it was a little late in the day to be worrying about the way both articles of clothing hugged the slenderness of her figure, clearly outlining the gentle curve of her hips and breasts.

David said nothing about the alteration to her hair or the addition of the glasses as she joined him in the tiny lounge a few minutes later, although she knew by the way his dark blue gaze flickered over her that he had noticed the changes in her appearance. Her cheeks instantly warmed.

'I've put enough coal on the fire to last until we get back,' he told her lightly as he opened the front door for her.

She had noticed the thoughtful action as soon as she came down the stairs. Another one of those 'nice' things about David Kendrick that were too dangerous for her peace of mind. And her need for privacy.

But, as if he were well aware now of how even so small an act could make her wary and suspicious, David seemed to deliberately leave her to her own thoughts on the drive into town, putting on an unintrusive cassette to alleviate the silence so that it shouldn't become too uncomfortable, perfectly relaxed himself as he sat capably behind the wheel of the Range Rover.

This man was worse than dangerous, he was lethal, and it was something she must never forget, despite his seemingly easygoing nature; he was a man determined to have his own way where she was concerned, with honey if he could manage it, but if not, by some other means. He hadn't become, and remained, successful in a cut-throat world like publishing was today, without learning how to be a survivor!

He remained just as unobtrusively in the background as Jade wandered around the supermarket, pushing the trolley along for her after insisting he could at least do that.

It was worth losing that particular battle just for the pleasure of seeing the head of Empire Publishing trying to control an errant shopping trolley up and down the shop's aisles—*that* seemed one battle he was doomed to fail at as he constantly crashed into either the laden shelves or other poor shoppers.

Jade, walking a short distance ahead of him as she perused the shelves, had difficulty containing her mirth as David let out yet another expletive before impatiently righting the trolley on to a straight path—for about two seconds! To give credit where it was due, David was being wonderfully patient, but that didn't make the whole scene any less funny.

She paused at a stand where a specialised saleslady was trying to market a new cheese spread, giving David time to partially win his battle and catch up with her. The cheese spread didn't taste as nice as others she had tried in the past, and, smiling a polite refusal at the other woman as she tried to sell her a jar, she turned to continue her shopping.

'Perhaps your husband would care to try some?' the woman prompted hastily as she realised she wasn't about to make a sale after all, despite her avid sales talk.

'I don't——'

'I'd love to,' David answered the other woman warmly.

Jade turned slowly, just in time to see David pop one of the small crackers smeared with the cheese spread into his mouth.

He chewed it around thoughtfully. 'Very nice,' he nodded, turning to Jade, pure devilment in his eyes. 'Try it again, darling, and see what you think,' he encouraged softly.

Irritation darkened her eyes; David had no right to deceive the poor saleswoman into thinking they were actually going to buy some of the awful spread, and he certainly had no right to let her go on thinking they were husband and wife! 'But we aren't——'

'Into cheese, I know,' David completed smoothly—and completely incorrectly; he knew damn well she had been about to vehemently deny they were husband and wife. 'But I think you'll agree,' he bestowed a heart-stopping smile on the middle-aged saleslady, 'that these are delicious.' He indicated the crackers on the display table.

They were no such thing, and they *all* knew it, even the other woman looking a little surprised by his enthusiasm. She was obviously only employed on a temporary basis until the product had been introduced to the general public, probably having to try and sell a different product—just as awful as this one!—every week. All the more reason not to lead the poor woman on now.

Jade's mouth twisted. 'I don't think this is one of those occasions, David, when there's a hidden camera all prepared to get you on film and put you on television next week!'

He grinned, unabashed. 'Try it again, sweetheart. For me,' he encouraged throatily.

She would 'sweetheart' him right around his— No, she abhorred physical violence, remember, and David's discoloured eye still showed the signs of her last lapse; she wondered what the saleslady thought of that! Besides, her last lapse had ended up with David announcing he was going to marry her!

She strolled back over to David's side, giving him a vengeful smile. 'I just wanted to explain that you aren't my husband,' she drawled calmly.

'I'm so sorry,' the flustered saleswoman apologised for her mistake. 'I didn't—I just thought——'

'I'm sure you aren't really interested in our living arrangements,' David cut in lightly. 'Which reminds me, darling,' he turned back to Jade, his expression innocent, 'we ran out of washing-up liquid this morning.'

Her mouth tightened as he neatly turned the tables on her once more. Why was she even bothering to challenge him in this way? It was a foregone conclusion that she would lose.

To give David his due, he did actually purchase a jar of the cheese spread before they left, leaving behind them one satisfied saleslady—even if the jar was likely to go straight in the bin once they got back to the cottage!

David began to chuckle as they loaded the shopping into the back of the Range Rover. 'It was worth the eighty pence to watch you squirm for a change,' he explained at her questioning look.

'Sorry?' she frowned at him.

'You looked as if you were about to explode with laughter in there a couple of times,' he nodded in the direction of the supermarket. 'While I played

ten-pin-bowling with the other shoppers!' He gave
a rueful grin.

She smiled in spite of herself. 'Some trolleys do
seem to have a will of their own.'

'This one certainly did,' he pushed it into one of
the appropriate lanes in the car park with obvious
relief. 'Changed your mind about the Christmas
tree?' he prompted gently as he rejoined her.

It unsettled her slightly that he didn't arrogantly
insist she had to have a tree; if he had she would
have lost no time in telling him 'no'! But, although
he was the type of man who liked things done, she
had also learnt that he wasn't the type who walked
all over other people's wishes. And she could see
that if she said she was still set on not having a tree
then he wouldn't press the issue. Which instantly
made her feel churlish for refusing in the first place.
Besides, she couldn't run away from memories for
the rest of her life.

'Why not?' she accepted lightly. 'But it will have
to be a small one,' she added hastily, not willing
to give in completely.

David nodded consideringly, laughter in the navy
blue eyes. 'I think it might get a little draughty in
the cottage if you had a ten-foot one sticking up
through the roof!'

Jade gave him a narrow-eyed glare, not deigning
to answer as she walked off.

Despite her earlier comments about the imprac-
ticality of real Christmas trees, she opted for one
of those rather than one of the plastic ones. There
were some really lovely artificial ones on sale in the

shops, but that was the trouble really, they *were* artificial, and, painful as the memories were, she had been used to the real pine-shedding type all her life, and couldn't break with that tradition.

After much deliberation they settled on a really bushy tree, about four feet high, which easily fitted into the back of the Range Rover. And then, of course, they had to go back to another big store to get the decorations for it.

It was while David was extolling the virtues of a rather large metallic red ball that could be hung from the ceiling that Jade spotted the mother of one of her pupils watching them a short distance away with open curiosity.

That was all Jade needed, although perhaps it was inevitable she should be recognised by someone in town; most of the people from the surrounding area shopped in town on Saturdays, and it was probably only the fact that the bad weather had kept some of them away that had saved her from a confrontation like this earlier in the morning.

'Mrs Shepherd,' she made a point of greeting the other woman before smiling down at the little girl at her side. 'Hello, Tracy. Are you busy getting things for your tree, too?'

'Miss Mellors,' Tracy's mother greeted while Tracy herself shyly held up the pretty silver tinsel she had been busy choosing. 'Awful weather, isn't it?' Heather Shepherd added conversationally.

Jade smiled in acknowledgement, at the same time realising that David had noticed her transfer of interest and was watching them politely. 'Mrs

Shepherd, this is our headmaster's younger brother, David,' she introduced distantly. 'He's staying with the Kendricks for the holidays,' she supplied economically, her mouth twisting with rueful acceptance as she saw the avid interest in the other woman's face now that she knew David's identity. 'He very kindly offered to bring me into town today because of the bad weather,' she felt compelled to add.

'Actually, it's more a case of Penny wanting me out of the way because I was getting under her feet,' David confided charmingly as he shook the other woman's hand firmly.

Mrs Shepherd gave a wry smile. 'I know the feeling; it's so hectic this time of the year.'

'But worth it,' David said gently as he smiled down at Tracy, whose huge blue eyes dominated her pretty little face, and whose hair, a mass of jet-black curls, cascaded down her back.

Much like the little girl he and Sara might have had together, if only Sara had lived to give him a child...

It was so easy, with his lazily teasing nature, to forget that David had already known so much tragedy in his life. It was to his credit that he hadn't grown bitter from the blow life had dealt him so early in his life.

'Well, we must get on,' the little girl's mother excused. 'Tracy wants to go and see Father Christmas before we go home,' she confided indulgently.

'But I thought you saw him yesterday?' David teased as he went down on his haunches so that he should no longer tower over the shy little girl. Tracy held up one slender wrist, showing off the brightly coloured bracelet she had obviously received as her present from 'Father Christmas' the day before. 'It's beautiful,' he dutifully admired the piece of jewellery she obviously cherished. 'I know why you have to see him again.' He smiled at her mischievously. 'You left something off that enormous list you gave him yesterday!'

Tracy gave a coy giggle, waving shyly as her mother prepared to leave.

'If the list gets much bigger, the attic will collapse under the weight,' Mrs Shepherd told them in a whisper before moving off.

'I remember.' David straightened with a companionable grin Jade couldn't resist sharing. 'I envy you, you know,' he sighed wistfully. 'You must get a tremendous satisfaction working with children as lovely as that one all day,' he explained at her questioning look, still watching Tracy, the little girl sending him another shy wave every now and then as she made her way to the cash-till with her mother.

'I do love my work,' Jade nodded. 'But the children all have their moments!'

He turned with an understanding laugh. 'In other words, they can be little devils when they choose. Even Tracy.' He resumed choosing the decorations.

'Even Tracy,' she agreed lightly. 'Although I have to admit, she's usually good.'

David decided to have the large red ball after all, placing it in the basket with the other things they had already chosen. 'I guess my Father Christmas yesterday wasn't enough to satisfy them until the big night,' he grimaced. 'Although at least now I know who—and what—takes up that space at the end of your bed,' he said self-mockingly.

'Wellington,' she acknowledged drily.

He nodded. 'I plagued poor Penny for hours yesterday to tell me if there was a special man in your life.' He frowned as a closed look came over her face. 'Don't look like that; Penny was the soul of discretion if there was anything to tell, told me to ask *you* any personal questions like that. Although she would admit there had been no one that she knew of during the few months since you've been here,' he murmured thoughtfully. 'Does that mean there's someone in London?'

Jade had stiffened as soon as he mentioned the possibility of there being a man in her life, the easy camaraderie that had developed during the morning rapidly fading as her barriers moved firmly back into place.

David gave a pained grimace at her tight-lipped expression. 'Penny was right, that question was obviously too personal even to ask you.' He took the shopping basket out of her unresisting fingers. 'I think we have enough decorations here now.'

She nodded abruptly. 'It's only a small cottage.' Her voice was strained.

He went to move away, stopped, turning back with a sigh. 'I'm sorry if I've upset you with my questions.' He shook his head in regret. 'I was really enjoying spending this day with you.'

So had she been, until that timely reminder. She had briefly forgotten the reason she chose to distance herself from people, the reason she dared not let anyone close to her, even a man like David who she knew without a doubt was good and kind. But she had remembered all too well now her reasons for remaining apart from such friendships, would have to take care she didn't forget again.

For to forget again, to allow herself the indulgence of this man's warmth, was a danger to her, and to everything she had so painstakingly built up for herself in the last year and a half.

The tragedy in David's past had been tremendous, but her own loss had been almost as great, although luckily no one had died. But she had lost. And she had sacrificed. At the time it had all been more than she had thought she could humanly bear.

She dared not leave herself open to that type of pain again.

She couldn't have guessed then, as her spine stiffened with resolve, how soon the fragile world she had managed to build for herself was to be completely shattered...

CHAPTER FIVE

IT WAS difficult to remain distant and unmoved in the face of David's boyish enthusiasm for putting up the decorations and the tree.

But she tried very hard to do just that as the homely cottage was transformed into a glittering world of Christmas fantasy, everywhere she looked a dazzling reminder of the festive season soon to come. Achingly haunting memories surfaced just at the sight of them, causing a painful lump in her throat.

'What do you think, Wellington?' David stepped back from the tree he had just brought inside, firmly established in a bucket of earth, the cat having sat on the hearthrug watching him in fascinated curiosity during the whole procedure of putting up the other decorations. 'Is it straight in the bucket?' He glanced down at the cat, Wellington staring back at him with unblinking green eyes, his head tilted questioningly to one side. 'No, I didn't think it was, either,' David sighed, moving to adjust the trunk of the tree in the bucket of earth.

Jade had been standing in the kitchen doorway listening all the time this one-sided conversation had been taking place, shaking her head ruefully at David's idiocy. 'A little more to the right,' she advised softly as he stared at the tree frustratedly.

He instantly turned to the cat in feigned wonderment. 'You talked,' he pounced. 'My God, Wellington, you could make a fortune going around showing you're the only talking cat ever known to mankind. Of course, we'll have to break it to Jade gently that she's been wrong about your sex all this time, but——'

'Very funny,' Jade drawled drily as she strolled fully into the room.

'Oh, it was you all the time,' he said with mock surprise. 'You've been so quiet since we got back that I felt sure your voice must have gone.'

She ignored the gently questioning gibe, knowing that, although he would understand her feelings of desolation this time of year if she cared to explain, she wouldn't do so. Eighteen months ago she wouldn't have believed herself capable of such distant withdrawal from human closeness; it had just been a lesson she had learnt the hard way.

But the silence between David and herself was companionable now as they adorned the tree, David handing her the angel to put on the top as the final decoration. Jade felt a lump in her throat as David flicked the electricity switch and the gaily coloured lights trailed around the tree were illuminated.

'Thank you,' was all she could say huskily, but she could see by the warmth in navy blue eyes that David understood her emotion.

'Now, how about a late lunch before driving over to see Penny and Simon?' he suggested briskly. 'I told them when I telephoned earlier that I hoped to spend the day with you, and Penny invited us over for tea with them and the children if we cared to go.'

Jade stiffened. 'And you accepted for me?'

'No,' he gently calmed her. 'I told her we would let her know.'

She relaxed slowly. 'I'm sorry.' She felt churlish for jumping to conclusions, wishing he would stop being so damned nice so that she might at least start distrusting him again. Because that mistrust had taken a serious blow today.

David stepped forward, standing just in front of her, long slender hands coming up to cradle either side of her face. 'Whoa,' he gentled softly as she would have jerked away. 'I only wanted to thank you for our time together today,' he explained huskily.

She became still, blinking up at him, her eyes deeply puzzled.

'It's the best time I've had in years,' he told her gruffly, the warmth of his gaze caressing her. 'I really felt as if I "belonged" here with you today. It's the feeling I've missed the most.'

She knew exactly what he meant by the term— the feeling of being a couple, of sharing. It was something she too had known once, something she too had missed, even though she had tried to block it from her mind, something she too had felt briefly between them today. Dangerous, dangerous, *dangerous*...

That danger came even closer as David lowered his head towards her, navy blue depths holding her captive before his head had lowered enough for his lips to touch and know hers.

Electrified satin. It was a contradiction in terms, but it was the only way Jade could think of to describe what it was like to be kissed by this man. The feeling washed over her so completely that she couldn't help but be captivated by the contrasting touch. David's lips against hers were like satin, but tiny shivers of tingling pleasure made Jade's mouth throb, almost like tiny electric shocks.

Electrified satin...

Jade swayed dizzily towards him, clasping his forearms to stop herself from moulding her body against his. She couldn't, she just couldn't!

David instantly released her as he felt that slight resistance. 'I'll build up the fire while you go up and get your change of clothes for this evening,' he told her huskily. 'You haven't forgotten Penny and Simon are throwing a party tonight?' he prompted lightly at her lack of response, acting for all the world as if that kiss had never happened.

But Jade had forgotten everything in the midst of that kiss, even her name very briefly! What *was* her name?

'Jade?' he prompted again, his expression indulgent at her dazed reaction.

Oh, yes—Jade. Dear God, David wasn't the one that was insane, *she* was. She had enjoyed his lips against hers, found pleasure in the protection they seemed to give her, had actually wanted the kiss to continue, had had to force herself to make it stop.

'Your change of clothes,' he reminded her lightly before turning towards the fire.

Jade continued to watch the broadness of his back for several seconds as he put coal on the fire as professionally as he had this morning, shaking herself to clear the fog from her numbed brain before quickly hurrying from the room. She sat down shakily on her bed.

Madness, utter madness. And the greatest madness of all was that she knew the cottage was going to seem very lonely now that it had known David's presence...

None of her distress at that knowledge was obvious when she came down the stairs a short time later, having changed the denims for black tailored trousers but left on the dark green jumper. She carried the clothes she intended wearing that evening in a bag.

She coolly met David's gaze as he turned from stroking Wellington to look at her. 'I'll feed him before we go, and then go and check on Cleo,' she told him distantly.

His brows rose. 'Another pet?'

Jade turned back at his puzzled query, a half-smile on her lips. 'My car,' she corrected drily.

'Oh,' he straightened, with a rueful grimace for the mistake he had made.

She nodded briskly. 'I just want to run the engine for a while.'

'It's a good idea to charge up the battery in such severe weather,' he nodded.

She could see that although he approved of that idea he found the idea of a car named Cleo a little on the strange side!

'Personally,' he continued, straight-faced, 'I call mine George!' He grinned.

She gave a relaxed laugh, any moments of tension that might have existed completely gone. She went into the kitchen with a rueful shake of her head.

David went to put her things in the back of the Range Rover while she opened the garage doors to turn the engine over on the car.

He came in to lean on the open window a short time later. 'It looks in good condition,' he admired, smoothing a hand over the perfect paintwork.

'*She* is,' Jade corrected pointedly, revving up the engine. 'I've had her six years now and she's never let me down yet. Her previous owner—and he was the original—said she had never let him down either. She's getting a bit old,' she realised affectionately. 'But I'll keep her until she falls apart now. What's George?' It felt good to be on such a safe topic as their respective vehicles after what had happened earlier!

'A Jag,' he admitted softly. 'Sports model.'

'Don't apologise for it,' she teased his near reluctance to own up to such a powerful and expensive car. 'I just happen to be rather attached to my Mini.'

'A cat and a car,' he remarked thoughtfully. 'There must be room in there for me somewhere!' he added with self-mockery.

The revving of the engine came to an abrupt halt as she took her foot off the accelerator to switch off the ignition, climbing out of the car to put an abrupt end to the conversation too. 'Shall we go?' she prompted stiltedly, her expression remote.

In truth, although she did like to check on Cleo in severe weather like this, most of the reason for her delay was a reluctance to see Penny and Simon after having spent the day with David in spite of her previous hostility towards him.

She could feel her tension mounting as they approached the house, David having accepted her earlier rebuff with good grace, music playing softly on the radio to alleviate the pointed silence.

The presence of 'George' parked in the driveway beside Penny's estate car momentarily diverted her attention away from her own dilemma, a sleek, dark grey car whose lines cried out its distinctive make.

'George,' she admired mockingly as she stepped out on to the driveway.

David ran a hand lovingly down the sleek bonnet. 'The one and only. I can't claim to have had him as long as you've had Cleo, but *I'm* very attached to him.'

Once again their conversation about their ridiculously personally named cars helped to ease the tension between them. 'A family who loves you, a beautiful car—what more could you possibly want?' Jade teased lightly, instantly wishing she hadn't as his expression became wistful. 'I didn't mean——'

'I know you didn't.' He squeezed her arm reassuringly. 'But don't worry, I've found what it is I "want".'

'David——'

'Now don't get yourself in a panic,' he calmed her. 'I'm not in any hurry.'

She shook her head. 'But I can't——'

'You don't have to do anything, Jade,' he soothed gently. 'I have to admit that my first instinct was to take you away somewhere, lock you up until you—Jade?' His bantering tone turned to one of concern as she paled. 'God, what did I say?' he frowned worriedly. 'Jade, tell me what I——'

'I'm all right.' She waved away his concern as the front door of the house was swung open, two children bounding impatiently down the steps to greet them.

Jade had met the two Kendrick boys before, had always thought them to be eleven- and twelve-year-old versions of their father, but as they launched themselves excitedly at their uncle she could see it was David they most resembled, their eyes as dark a blue as his, the boys themselves so much alike, with their tall, gangling bodies and untidy mops of dark hair, that they could almost be mistaken for twins.

David was obviously pleased to see his young nephews again too, returning their exuberant hugs, although his worried gaze searched Jade's face before she turned pointedly away.

Jade was glad of the diversion of the Kendrick children during the next half an hour. Neither of the boys were satisfied until they had shown their uncle their bedrooms and then taken him out to the garage to show him the bicycles they had received for their birthdays earlier in the year; Jade had received a jolt she needed time to recover from.

'Was it that bad?' Penny prompted gently at her side after all the male members of the family had been persuaded to disappear outside to the garage. She shook her head reprovingly. 'I thought David was rushing things a little when he rang earlier to say he hoped to be with you all day. The trouble with David is he never learnt any patience,' she added crossly. 'I would have felt like hitting him if he had dared to wake me up at seven o'clock in the morning for a snowball fight.' Her mouth quirked with amusement as she could visibly see Jade's tension begin to relax into a rueful smile. 'Hugging him a little, too, I think,' she admitted affectionately. 'He can be the most infuriating man!'

Yes, he could. But he could also be kind. And thoughtful. And dangerous to her peace of mind. And it was the latter she had to remember.

By the time the other members of the family returned, and she and Penny were dragged into a boisterous game of Monopoly, she had almost forgotten that moment of sheer panic she had experienced when she and David had first arrived here. Almost...

'Penny hasn't lost her ability to throw a successful party,' David drawled on the drive back to her cottage several hours later.

It had been a pleasant evening, most of the people there familiar to Jade. What had made it slightly uncomfortable for her was the interest all of Penny and Simon's friends had taken in Simon's brother. As David's obvious partner for the evening—no matter how much she might have wished it didn't appear that way!—she had come in for considerable interest herself. No doubt a lot of those people had believed her to have moved very fast to capture David's interest in that way! To his credit, David had made very sure everyone knew he more than returned any interest she might feel.

'I can't get over how much the boys have grown.' He gave a rueful shake of his head. 'They were only seven and eight the last time I spent any time with them,' he admitted heavily. 'I've missed them both so much,' he added gruffly.

The boys had obviously missed their uncle too, even though four years must have seemed a very long time in their young lives.

But at least now Jade had some idea of how long David's wife had been dead. And the four years had seemed even longer to him than it had to the boys, because he had had nothing left in his life.

'I should have known not to play Monopoly against you,' Jade derided, lightly changing the subject. 'I had forgotten that I once read about you that you're considered the "entrepreneur with the Midas touch"; a little game like Monopoly was child's play to you!'

He grinned in the half-light, several small street-lamps illuminating the small village. 'Simon and I always used to win when we played as children.' He gave her a teasing look. 'Simon was better at it than me, if anything; in fact, he would have been a more successful businessman than me if he had chosen to go into that profession instead of teaching.'

'He's an excellent headmaster,' Jade told him quietly.

'Even better than he would have been a businessman,' David nodded. 'I'm sure he gets a lot more satisfaction out of it, too,' he frowned.

She gave him a curious look. 'You sound almost—disillusioned?'

'Not really,' he shrugged with a sigh. 'I just—— Sometimes I wish I could have done something that made me feel—more fulfilled. Useful, I suppose I mean.'

'But the books you publish fulfil a lot of people's lives,' Jade protested.

'So why not mine?' he accepted. 'I've been searching——' He glanced at her. 'But I really think that time is over for me now,' he said with satisfaction.

She swallowed hard. 'David——'

'They're really on their toes around here,' he murmured, his attention briefly on the driving mirror to the side of his normal vision. 'You're either a very dangerous lot or they have a serious drink-driving problem in this area,' he teased.

She blinked at him, disconcerted by the sudden change of subject. 'Sorry?'

'We have another police car behind us.' He nodded in the direction of the blazing lights visible in his mirror. 'They joined us a few minutes ago.'

Jade turned in her seat to look at the car, quickly swinging back again to lean weakly against the head-rest behind her. Twice in as many days—*could* it be a coincidence still? And if not, what could they want with her after all this time?

'Uh-oh,' David groaned, and Jade tensed anew. 'They just turned off to follow another car; I hope the driver hasn't even looked at alcohol!'

Thank God they had gone! This was ridiculous, she hadn't felt this hounded in a very long time. And she wished she didn't have to feel that way now.

And yet the incident had thrown her again; what had been quite a pleasant evening was now shrouded in uncertainty, leaving her restless and ill at ease.

Wellington got up from his place in front of the fading fire to leave the room with a disgusted flick of his tail as soon as they entered the cottage.

'He's annoyed because I've been out two evenings in a row and left him all alone,' Jade murmured ruefully as the cat walked unhurriedly up the stairs.

David smiled. 'I would be pretty annoyed myself in the same circumstances.'

'Coffee?' she prompted brittly; after all, it was what he had come in for!

'Please,' he nodded, not in the least perturbed by her sudden frost, already moving to build up the fire.

He had made himself quite considerably 'at home' in the cottage the last couple of days, Jade recognised moodily as she prepared the coffee, and it wasn't a feeling she was comfortable with. In fact, she had been uncomfortable about one thing or another ever since she had first met David Kendrick!

She was even more disconcerted when she went back into the sitting-room to find the only illumination in the now cosily warm room was the glowing fire and the small coloured lights on the Christmas tree. And with the tray of coffee taking up both her hands, there wasn't a thing she could immediately do to remedy the intimacy!

David seated himself beside her on the sofa, his smile so innocent it couldn't possibly be sincere. 'All right.' He sat back defeatedly as she continued to look at him, her brows raised. 'It's not very subtle. But then, I didn't think you were in the mood to appreciate subtlety.' He grimaced. 'I can see now that you aren't in the mood to appreciate the "bang on the head" approach either!'

He was so bluntly honest, had been from the beginning, and he looked so much like a little boy caught with his hand inside the 'cookie jar', that Jade couldn't help but smile, the smile turning to a chuckle as he gave a cross-eyed look of self-derision.

They shared a warm smile as Jade poured out the coffee, their silence companionable as they sat drinking the hot brew in the quiet of the room, gazing at the beauty of the glittering Christmas tree.

'You'll have to help me a little and tell me what *will* induce you to come into my arms,' David suddenly groaned. 'Because I'm not sure how much longer I can wait to hold you!'

Jade turned to him sharply, frowning at the expression of pained longing in his eyes, feeling a sudden light-headedness as she swayed towards him.

It was the sign he had been waiting for, all the encouragement he needed; his arms were firm and warm about her, not imprisoning, but not about to release her either unless she demanded he do so. Which she didn't.

Electrified satin... It hadn't been her imagination this afternoon, nor indeed been blown out of proportion in her distress.

Electrified satin...

There could be no doubt about it, nor the fact that her reaction to his touch was just as volatile as it had been earlier. And just as insane. But this time she was unable to stop his kisses and caresses. Unable to deny David—or herself...

He felt so good to touch, the softness of the material of his shirt doing nothing to hide the hardness of his body beneath, her fingertips moving tentatively up his chest to his shoulders, clinging there as the smoothness of his lips moved to the fluttering column of her throat, his tongue probing moistly.

Oh, God, the sensation, the raw, burning sensation, unlike anything she had ever known before. Her throat arched as his lips moved in a downward path, pushing aside the high collar of her dress to probe the sensitive hollows beneath with moist pleasure.

Briefly, so very briefly, she tried to resist the questing hand that trailed lightly across the soft curve of her breasts, but it was only briefly and she groaned low in her throat as gentle fingers slowly parted the top three buttons of her dress.

That same hand burnt her flesh as his fingers rested above the soft curve of her breasts, not moving, just burning her with its warmth.

Their mouths fused, clinging damply together, moving together in erotic rhythm, Jade whimpering longingly with a need to know the full touch of that hand that still lay so hotly against her.

'David,' she gasped when their mouths parted. 'Please!' she voiced her need, moving impatiently against him. 'Why don't you—what are you waiting for?' she groaned in half-pain as he still made no effort to touch her more intimately, her body throbbing with a need to know that touch.

He closed lids over darkened blue eyes, wincing as he opened them again. 'Your cat to get his claws out of my thigh!' he told her calmly.

Jade blinked up at him dazedly for several seconds, the full impact of what he had just said not hitting her. And even when it did she still looked up at him disbelievingly, glancing down at his legs to see that Wellington did indeed have his claws stuck in David's flesh—and he didn't look as if he intended removing them in the near future, either!

'Good God!' she gasped as she struggled to sit up. 'Don't move,' she advised worriedly as she began the delicate operation of removing Wellington.

David's mouth quirked in spite of the pain he was in. 'I don't intend to.'

As fast as Jade removed Wellington's claws from David's leg he put them back in again, seeming determined to maim the poor man.

'And I thought earlier that he had taken to me!' David winced as the claws dug into his flesh with renewed vigour. 'He certainly knows how to put a dampener on the mood.' He massaged his punctured flesh as Jade at last managed to release him and shoo the cat out of the room. 'I suppose Wellington was just trying to tell me that he'll let me so close and no further.'

A little as she had since the first moment they met! 'I'm sorry.' She shrugged uncomfortably, not knowing what else to say.

'I'm not.' David stood up to move away from her. 'I told you earlier, I'm in no hurry, and that includes trying to seduce you in front of glowing fires—romantic as the idea seems,' he added ruefully. 'We have time, Jade,' he told her seriously. 'And I don't intend rushing you one step of the way.'

When Jade found the footprints around the house and garage the next day in the fresh fall of snow, she wasn't sure she was going to be able to stay in the area, to be hurried or not!

The snow had fallen during the night while she'd slept so restlessly, and when she got up at seven o'clock the next morning no one had called at the cottage, it was still too early even for the milkman to come, and yet a brief walk outside to clear the cobwebs from her tired brain had revealed those footprints in the pure carpet of snow that covered the ground.

The coincidence of the police car following them two nights in a row instantly came to mind, her panic renewed even though they had made no effort to approach her either time. They didn't need to approach her, just to let her know they were there, and if she made a complaint no doubt they would have a ready excuse for being there; David's belief that they were looking for Christmas revellers who had over-indulged would no doubt be as good as any. But she knew that wasn't really the reason, just as well as the police did. Why had they started hounding her again after all this time; what more could they want from her that hadn't already been taken?

As she heard the seven-thirty news on the radio, she finally knew the answer to that . . .

CHAPTER SIX

'IT HAS now been disclosed by the police that three prisoners escaped while being transferred from one prison to another two days ago. Two of the men have since been recaptured, but a third man is still being hunted by police. No further details are available at this time.'

The announcement, slotted in so casually among other general news, was the sort of information most people would listen to and then dismiss, forget even, paying no further attention to such a trivial matter. What did it matter to the general public that one prisoner had managed to escape, a prisoner they didn't even feel it necessary to be called by name?

But Jade wasn't just any member of the general public, she knew the man's name, was sure beyond a shadow of a doubt that it was Peter. And the police were watching her because they believed either that she would know where he was or that he might actually come here.

She wouldn't take a single step to help him, she despised him with all the loathing that she was capable of! As for him searching her out, she had every reason to know he wouldn't do that, either.

But the police had never believed her version of what had happened, had tried for weeks to get her to admit to something she had no knowledge of. Peter's own testimony that she hadn't been involved had done little to convince them, either. Not that she had wanted or welcomed his help anyway, she'd been so disgusted with him by then, hating him for using her to hurt others.

As he continued to hurt her. God, she had begun to actually hope last night, to imagine she might finally be able to put the past behind her, to make a new life for herself, possibly with David. But, even if that third prisoner didn't turn out to be Peter, the incident had served as a reminder that the past was all she could ever have, that there could be no real future for her, with David or any other man.

Before David had left the evening before they had chuckled together about Wellington's jealous behaviour, Jade accepting his invitation to spend the day with the family without hesitation. She had even been anticipating the day she would spend with him!

He was such a good man, made her feel so special because that was what he was and he seemed to care about her. Why, oh, why couldn't she have even had just a few days' happiness with him? It might have been enough——

No, it wouldn't, because she had it inside her to care very deeply for David Kendrick, already did care more than she should.

And it was over now, over before it had ever really begun.

She listened to the news bulletin on the radio every half-hour after that until ten o'clock, but nothing was added to that particular news item, and as she saw the Range Rover turn into the driveway she switched the radio off, no longer willing to listen so anxiously, certainly not for David to see that anxiety.

Sadness darkened her eyes as she caught sight of the Christmas tree glittering in the corner of the room on her way to open the door to him. The tree no longer glowed magically as it had yesterday, no longer represented putting the past behind her. That romantic glow had been ripped from her eyes to leave only stark reality; now it just looked like a slightly misshapen tree covered in lots of gaudy ornaments and over-bright lights.

'Good morning, good morning,' David greeted cheerfully, cupping her face in his hands to kiss her lightly on the lips. 'Ten-fifteen on the dot,' he announced with satisfaction as he strode forcefully inside the cottage. 'I've been up and wanting to come over and see you since six o'clock, but resisted the impulse.' He gave a self-derisive laugh. 'The people that know me in London probably wouldn't believe my self-control; I'm not known for my reserve there.'

She could imagine he wasn't. He was a forceful, dynamic man who had forged an empire for himself by sheer self-will and determination. Probably those women, Christi and Dizzy, would have trouble believing his forbearance last night, too!

She couldn't help the jealousy that shot through her at the thought of the role the other two women had in his life.

'Dizzy and Christi would probably be amazed,' she said brittly.

He chuckled. 'I'm sure they would,' he acknowledged, without apology for talking of the other two women in his life, his grin one of pure devilment. 'They're going to be even more surprised when I tell them I intend marrying you as soon as I can persuade you to have me!'

She could imagine surprise wasn't all the other two women would feel if he were ever to make such an announcement!

Not that he ever would, of course; she would make very certain that he knew she never would 'have him' before he returned to London. His life had been in ruins once already, and she wouldn't allow it to happen to him a second time because of something in her past.

It was already too late to prevent herself being hurt; she knew now that she had started to love him!

How could she help it? David was everything any woman could possibly want. Everything. But there was one thing she was determined he would never be, and that was hurt by what had happened eighteen months ago. She wouldn't allow that to touch him.

'I'm not going with you today.' Her voice was gruffly abrupt as she forced the words out. 'I—I don't feel too well after yesterday,' she hastily invented as disappointment clouded his face. 'I think I must have caught a chill when we were out in the snow.'

Concern instantly darkened his ruggedly handsome face. 'God, I never thought—you shouldn't be out of bed if you feel ill,' he frowned, already taking a firm hold of her arm and marching her towards the stairs. 'I thought when I arrived that you looked a little pale, but I put that down to——'

'What do you think you're doing?' Jade gasped as they reached the top of the stairs and he gently pushed her towards her open bedroom door.

David gave her a mockingly chiding look, sitting her on the bed and going down on his haunches in front of her to take off her shoes. 'Helping you, nothing else,' he derided her alarm.

'But——'

'God, your feet are like blocks of ice!' he scolded, rubbing them between the warmth of his hands.

She had got her feet wet trudging out in the snow this morning, and they hadn't felt warm since, although she had felt little inclination to go and put dry socks on.

There was something very erotic about having David massage her feet in this way, and she pulled sharply away from him.

'Steady,' he reproved, not releasing her.

'There's no need for this,' her voice was harsh. 'I just have a chill——'

'I can feel that.' He wasn't in the least deterred by her dismissive attitude. 'I'm not surprised; it's freezing up here.' He looked about the tiny room censoriously.

'The heat from the fire downstairs hasn't quite reached this far yet——'

'I think the best thing to do is get you into bed and then I'll go down and check on the heating,' David murmured to himself, almost as if she hadn't spoken—which she might just as well not have done, for all the notice he was taking of her. 'I'm not sure you should stay on here anyway if you aren't feeling well.' He shook his head.

Her eyes widened. 'Of course I'm staying here——'

'The heating is unpredictable at best,' he continued as if she still hadn't voiced a protest. 'And you can't possibly keep the fire going if you're ill up here in bed. I think it would be best if I took you back with me to the house——'

Jade gasped. 'I have no intention——'

'Unless, of course, you'll agree to the idea of my moving in here for a few days to take care of you?' He looked at her with mocking eyes. 'Just until you get over the worst of it.'

'It's only a slight chill, David,' she cut in firmly. 'Not enough to incapacitate me, just enough to make me feel slightly unsociable.' God, she wished she had never started the deception of the chill now; it was bringing more problems than it was solving! 'I'll be perfectly all right here on my own, in fact I would prefer it.' How she would prefer it! The idea was to get him out of her life, to keep him out, not to have him actually move in here with her!

The look David gave her told her he was perfectly well aware of her preference for being alone.

'I couldn't possibly leave you here alone when you aren't well,' he dismissed briskly. 'No matter what you would prefer,' he added as she seemed about to protest again.

She wanted to tell him she didn't care what *he* couldn't possibly do, but she knew from experience that David was perfectly capable of ignoring her, that he was already doing so, turning back the duvet and plumping up the pillows ready for her to get into bed.

'David...' Her voiced trailed off lamely as his brows rose silencingly. 'But I don't want to go to bed,' she sighed her impatience.

'The story of my life,' he drawled mockingly.

'Very funny,' she grimaced her irritation with his humour. 'I'll be perfectly all right if I just spend the day sitting quietly in front of the fire. There's no need to spoil everyone's day,' she told him determinedly.

'My day isn't being spoilt,' he dismissed easily. 'And Penny would never forgive me if I didn't take proper care of you.'

'I'll forgive you——'

'Besides,' David added teasingly, 'what would all your neighbours think of my concern for your welfare yesterday if today I calmly drive off and leave you when I know you're ill?'

'None of my neighbours know that I feel ill,' she protested exasperatedly.

'*I* know,' he mocked chidingly. 'Now get into this bed and stop being argumentative.'

Maybe if she just got into bed and pretended to be asleep he would go away and leave her alone! She could definitely add stubborn to that description of nice, and the two together were an unstoppable combination.

'Do you usually go to bed fully clothed?' he drawled as she lay down on the smooth sheet.

'When there's a man in my bedroom, yes!' She very firmly pulled up the duvet, glaring at him over the top of it.

David grinned down at her, his arms folded across the width of his chest. 'How often have you gone to bed in your clothes?'

Her mouth pursed. 'In other words, how often have I had a man in my bedroom?'

He raised innocent brows. 'I wouldn't presume to ask such a question.'

'That's good, because I have no intention of answering it, either!' Jade muttered, settling herself more comfortably beneath the warmth, not looking at him again as she pointedly closed her eyes.

She could sense his mocking gaze on her for several more minutes before he quietly left the room. She listened intently for the sound of the door closing as he left the cottage, the start of the Range Rover's engine. What she did hear was the tiny ting of the telephone as he picked up the receiver to make a call, followed by the soft murmur of his voice, and then silence. Absolute silence.

Damn it, he had really meant it about not leaving. She should have known that he wouldn't be affected by her feigning sleep—it had probably made him all the more determined to stay on!

She moved over on her back to stare up at the ceiling in silent frustration.

She had wanted to be alone today, to wait for—whatever. There would eventually be news of that third prisoner, there had to be, and whether it was Peter or not, she really needed to be alone when that happened.

If the police didn't come here first. That was always a possibility. They had kept away so far, simply keeping a silent watch on her and the cottage, but that couldn't continue if the prisoner really was Peter, as she believed it was.

The trembling she had known this morning, when she'd first heard the news, returned. She had thought this fear, at least, had gone from her life. Maybe it would never really be over for her, she would certainly never be able to forget that dark shadow that dogged her life. This incident, no matter what the outcome, had shown her that.

'You're supposed to be sleeping,' David chided as he put his head around the side of the door and saw her lying there on the bed wide-eyed, entering the room fully to look down at her reprovingly. 'You—my God, you're shivering,' he realised with concern, moving to sit on the side of the bed, taking hold of her hands in his.

Her hands did feel chilled, but she certainly wasn't shivering with cold; David had seen her trembling, and to correct him in his assumption would be to arouse his curiosity about that trembling, and the reason behind it.

At the moment he was preoccupied with her condition. 'Maybe I should call the doctor——'

'Don't be silly,' Jade dismissed impatiently, her pulse-rate giving a lurch at the suggestion; a doctor would soon spot her symptoms for what they were; fear, not the 'flu. 'If you called a doctor out every time you had a chill, the poor man would never be in his surgery. And there isn't a lot he can do for the condition.'

'Maybe not,' David conceded with a frown. 'Maybe a hot drink would help,' he murmured, half to himself. 'It certainly couldn't do any harm,' he said scowlingly, obviously worried about her as he went over to the doorway. 'Don't move,' he warned sternly.

She had no intention of going anywhere, was too comfortable, the warmth beneath the duvet finally reaching her, and she wriggled more fully beneath the covering with a weary sigh of satisfaction.

Maybe she didn't really have a chill, but the shock of that news item on the radio had certainly shaken her up. Added to the tiredness she felt after her restless night, it wasn't surprising she felt so exhausted.

So exhausted she didn't hear David return with the hot drink because she had fallen into a deep sleep...

*   *   *

The eyes. All staring. Accusing. Everywhere she looked those eyes stared back at her. Disgust. Accusation. All of them hostile.

Except one pair. Navy blue eyes caressed her warmly, loved her, wanted her, embraced her. She ran towards those eyes, towards the warmth they offered, towards the arms that now reached out to her.

But as she reached those arms they began to disappear, to dissolve, and the warmth to fade with them, leaving only the cold loneliness.

'Don't go,' she sobbed pleadingly. 'Oh, please, don't go.' Her arms reached out in desperate need. 'David!' she cried his name, knowing he was the source of that warmth.

'Jade...' Those warm arms enfolded her now, gathering her close. 'Jade, I'm here.'

She clung to him, sighing her shaky relief when he didn't disappear beneath her touch, resting against him as she slowly relaxed, knowing she was safe now, that David wouldn't hurt her, ever.

She had had the strangest dream—frightening, oppressive. She had wanted to escape, to get out of the fear, but she hadn't been able to break free, had had to live through the nightmare.

And then the warmth had come, an engulfing warmth that still comforted her and held her. She settled more comfortably against that warmth, her nose twitching as the softness of wool tickled her.

Jade pushed the irritant away, feeling the hardness beneath her hand as she did so, puzzled by it but reluctant to relinquish the last hold she had on sleep and the lingering feelings of warmth she had so briefly known. Feelings so long denied her she was afraid to give them up now in case she never had them again, her eyes closed against the intruding outside world.

But the puzzle of that hardness beneath wool still troubled her, and even at the risk of losing the protective warmth she knew she had to open her eyes and solve that puzzle.

The warmth didn't fade as she raised her lids, but she was instantly lost in the navy blue depths above her, at last knowing what the woollen hardness was—a man's muscular chest!

'David...' she breathed wonderingly.

He nodded. 'I came to check on you because I could hear you moving about restlessly, and you asked me not to go,' he explained his presence apologetically, his face in shadow where he had pulled the curtains earlier against the daylight.

Jade remembered the dream, *David's* eyes welcoming her, wanting her, felt again the warmth his arms had offered, her fear that they would leave her. And they hadn't left her, *David* hadn't left her, was still holding her protectively against him, where the rest of the world couldn't touch her.

She smiled up at him tremulously. 'I'm glad I did.' Her eyes glowed with inner emotion.

Uncertainty flickered across the strength of his face. 'You aren't awake properly yet——'

'Because I'm not pushing you away?' she said self-derisively. 'Oh, I'm awake, David, completely awake. And I know exactly what I'm doing,' she added huskily as she slowly put her arms up about his neck and pulled him down to her.

He frowned down at her still. 'I'm not sure that you do——'

'David,' she rebuked firmly. 'Unless you don't want to kiss me?' she challenged, auburn brows arched questioningly over dark green eyes.

'Don't provoke me, Jade,' he sighed his impatience with her levity at a time when they should be so deadly serious.

Her expression softened, knowing he was hesitating for her sake, the hardness of his own body, the dark passion in his eyes, telling of his own need. And he had no need to hold back because of her; she knew that this was right between them. 'I just want you to make love to me,' she told him with simple honesty, her jade-green gaze unwavering.

His breath was sharply indrawn, and he shook his head. 'Don't think that just because we find ourselves in this—position,' he indicated the closeness of their bodies in the bed, 'it has to— lead—to anything.'

She smoothed the ruggedness of his cheek with gentle fingertips. 'If I didn't realise that your concern is for me, I could be quite hurt by your seeming reluctance to make love to me,' she teased.

'You know damn well that I——'

'I *do* know,' she soothed his explosive outburst. 'And I'm equally sure that this is what I want for myself,' she told him steadily.

He swallowed audibly. 'You are?'

'Yes.' She smiled with quiet confidence in her decision. 'And David,' she added softly, their lips only a fraction of an inch apart now, 'I've *never* gone to bed in my clothes before.'

His eyes glowed fiercely possessive at the admission she had made, his mouth moving to claim her sweetly before passion exploded between them and the sweetness turned to fiery need.

David was the lover she had been waiting for all her life, a man of strength and gentleness, rather than power and weakness, and she knew only pride in his gaze as he slowly removed the clothes that now seemed so unimportant to either of them, knowing what he would see, her high-breasted, narrow-waisted body a gift she had saved especially for him, although it had taken her until now to admit that even to herself.

But now she knew, her breasts fitting perfectly into his hands as his lips and tongue loved first one fiery tip and then the other before claiming them with heated moisture.

He was like a child against her, and yet the heat that engulfed her body could only come from this man, an aching need joining that heat to totally enslave and claim her.

She moved up on her knees on the bed beside him in a need to know the warmth of that hard body she had only touched through wool and denim, glorying in the male perfection of him as he helped her to remove his clothing, knowing the strength of their need for each other as his body trembled uncontrollably at her touch, the satin hardness pulsating with that need.

'You're so beautiful.' He caressed her with hands that trembled slightly.

'So are you,' she told him tremulously, no embarrassment or awkwardness between them, only beauty and emotion.

'I don't want to hurt you,' David breathed shakily as his mouth moved caressingly against her throat.

'You could never hurt me.' In that moment she had never been so sure of anything.

'I may not be able to prevent it,' he told her with husky regret.

'If there is pain, it will only be the kind that will bring pleasure,' she assured him softly. 'The pleasure of joining my body to yours.'

He drew in his breath raggedly. 'It's difficult to remain sane when you say things like that.'

'I don't want us to remain sane.' Jade gazed at him longingly.

'And lord knows I don't,' he muttered self-derisively.

'Then let's go quietly insane together.' She knelt proudly before him, her body beckoning.

They melded together perfectly as David came up beside her on the bed to heatedly claim her lips once more, the disparity in their heights when they were standing not apparent in that moment, breasts against a hard chest, their thighs cupped together perfectly, both of them aware only of the need they had to be just one flesh moving together in perfect harmony.

The pain, if it could be called that, lasted only briefly, unimportant, as that throbbing passion made their movements as beautiful as any ballet, a slow and tender building of pleasure until it was too late for tenderness and only throbbing need and burning desire remained, their movements frenzied now, desperate, climaxed by tiny cries of mutual pleasure found and received, their movements relaxing slowly before they fell damply together against the bedclothes.

Beautiful surrender, not just for her, but for David too. He had surrendered his heart as well as his body, and it was a moment Jade would cherish for the rest of her life. Because she had surrendered her heart, too.

How could any woman this man chose to love help but feel the same way?

And how long before she saw that light of love ripped from his eyes to be replaced by—what? Contempt? Disgust? Hate?

Dear God, she didn't think she could bear to see any of those emotions in eyes that had been misty with love!

As she saw Peter's photograph flash on the television screen as the third prisoner, the one the police were still searching for, later that evening, she knew she might not have any choice, that she was going to have to suffer through the nightmare again, and that this time there would be no David's arms to protect her warmly from those accusingly hostile eyes; once he knew the truth about her, his would probably be among them!

CHAPTER SEVEN

DAVID insisted on preparing her a light snack and serving it to her in bed, feeding her each mouthful of the fluffy golden eggs and toast, his arm supportive about her shoulders as she sipped the hot, sweet coffee, before he would even contemplate eating his own food.

And then he removed the tray from the bed between them and they made love again.

It was just as beautiful as before, made even more poignantly so for Jade because she had the inner knowledge that this would probably be her last time in his arms, her last chance to know the warmth he gave her.

That knowledge made it doubly difficult for her to be parted from him later that evening, and yet she knew she couldn't allow him to stay the night as he wanted to do; it was only a matter of time before the police no longer only watched from a distance. David accepted that they had her reputation to think of with the village people and also with Penny and Simon. It was no longer those things that worried Jade, but it was easier to let David go on believing it was.

'I don't want any clouds to mar our future happiness together.' He kissed her lingeringly on the lips as they stood close together in the living-room as he prepared to leave.

Pain darkened her eyes; after the encouragement she had given him today he no doubt felt he had more than a passing right to assume she was more open to his suggestion that they should get married. The truth of it was, she was even less open to that idea than ever before; at least before today she had been able to look on it as fanciful foolishness on his part; now she just knew the idea was totally impossible.

'No clouds.' David smoothed the frown from between her eyes. 'And no more doubts, either. You couldn't have made love to me the way you did if you didn't love me.'

It was true, all of it. She had made love to him, and she did love him.

He smiled gently down at her silence. 'I know, it's still too new to take in. But we have the rest of Christmas to get used to the idea, and in the New Year we can——'

'How you do love to make plans,' she teased huskily, her fingertips light against his hard cheek.

His smile became rueful. 'And how you do love to avoid them,' he chided.

Jade shrugged, moving slightly away from him, holding her robe wrapped tightly about her. 'I'm just not as impetuous as you are...'

He gave a soft chuckle. 'That's something else I'm not known for in the business world. You make me throw caution to the wind—but I suppose I can stop being so damned impatient now,' he announced cheerfully. 'We belong together, and we both know it.'

She swallowed hard. 'It's getting late,' she urged him, anxious to be alone now.

'At least Wellington has decided he likes me again now.' David moved down on his haunches to stroke the purring cat as he lay in front of the fire.

She didn't doubt that was because Wellington could see how happy David made her; the cat wasn't really in the least possessive, he just wanted a happy and contented mistress to feed him. Jade didn't walk around in a daze when she was happy. And she didn't forget to feed him then, either. And he even got titbits from her plate to eat when this man was about. Yes, Wellington had decided he liked him again.

She had never stopped liking him—that was the problem!

David straightened, moving to kiss her lightly on the lips. 'I wish I could stay... But I know I can't,' he accepted ruefully. 'So I'll be on my way.'

'Could I have—could I be alone tomorrow?' She looked at him with widely pleading eyes, knowing that if he insisted on seeing her she wouldn't be able to say no to him.

He looked down at her searchingly, his expression softening with love. 'Of course,' he readily agreed. 'But don't forget Penny is throwing one of her famous parties in the evening.'

She had forgotten, but it didn't matter. Almost twenty-four hours on her own should be enough to shore up her sadly depleted defences. Not that they would ever be quite that strong again, her love for David weakening her in a way she had hoped never to be weak again.

'I won't forget,' she nodded abruptly.

'Now I really had better go and let you get some rest.' He seemed to feel her distant behaviour was due to tiredness. 'A fine nurse I've made today,' he said ruefully. 'I've succeeded in tiring the patient out rather than letting her rest.'

Warm colour darkened her cheeks at the mischievous glitter in his eyes. 'All the more reason for me to have tomorrow on my own to recuperate,' she bit out tartly.

David held up his hands defensively. 'I've already conceded tomorrow,' he reminded her gently, his expression slightly reproachful.

She knew that; she just needed to assert some control, to re-establish that distance she needed to put herself back on that course of self-survival. If she could survive loving a man as wonderful as David and having to let him go...

'Get some sleep now.' He lightly grasped her arms to kiss her firmly on the lips. 'I'll call you tomorrow. Just to check how you are,' he defended ruefully at her frowning look, pulling on his jacket to tug the collar up about his neck and face against the driving snow that had begun to fall a short time ago.

Jade stood at the doorway and watched him go, anxious for these last glimpses of him, because by tomorrow—— Oh, God, she didn't want to think about tomorrow.

David turned back after he had gone only a few steps. 'Go back inside before you catch pneumonia,' he shouted against the wind that whistled about him in the icy darkness.

Flakes of snow were clinging to her hair and clothes, melting on the warmth of her face and hands, but she made no effort to move, watching until he had climbed into the Range Rover and driven off with a wave of his hand before turning back inside.

She closed the door slowly behind her, lost in her own thoughts, miserable thoughts of the loneliness she had to return to. She glanced down as she felt Wellington rub against her calf. 'Except for you, boy,' she choked as she bent to pick him up. 'No offence to you, darling,' she told him gruffly. 'But I don't think you're going to be enough any more.' Tears cascaded down her cheeks and into the snowy white fur as she hugged him to her, her face buried against his purring body. 'I love him, Wellington. I love him so much!' she sobbed brokenly, her control slipping completely.

How could she have come to love him so quickly, so deeply? How could she have allowed it to happen, for both their sakes? But she had needed— oh, God, how she had *needed*——

She gave a shaky sigh as Wellington seemed to look up at her reprovingly. 'I know, I was being selfish. I *am* selfish,' she groaned self-disgustedly, dropping down on to the sofa, her wind-tousled head thrown back against its softness, closing her eyes as the tears silently continued to fall.

The silence instantly closed in about her, with only the howling of the wind outside to alleviate the oppressive stillness that suddenly surrounded her.

She couldn't stand it, not when she had been surrounded by so much love and happiness since the moment she woke in David's arms, and she leaned forward abruptly to switch on the television set.

But that was little comfort either, the picture just flashing in front of her eyes, meaningless people who couldn't even begin to fill the sudden void in her life.

She had been staring at the photograph displayed on the screen behind the newsreader for some seconds before she realised that it was Peter. She scrambled forward on to the carpet to turn the sound up to an audible level, on her knees in front of the set as she heard confirmation of what she had already known within her heart.

'—it is hoped that, now the escaped man's name and photograph have been distributed by police, his capture will be forthcoming. And now we turn to the North of England, where——'

Jade no longer listened to what the attractive newscaster was saying, having heard all she needed to. She sat back on her heels with a sigh that was almost as heavy as the weight she now carried on her shoulders. The weight of guilt. Not for anything that had happened in the past—although goodness knew she had enough to blame herself for about that!—but for taking David's love so selfishly today.

She buried her face in her hands and wept.

David hadn't asked about past men in her life, although he had to know there had been some. But even if he had asked she couldn't have told him about Peter, a man she had loved with such joy that when she had learnt the shattering truth about him it had made it so much harder to bear.

David loved her with that same joy now, she was sure of it, even though the words had never been spoken. How much deeper he was going to be hurt when *this* all shattered about the two of them.

It was so easy to *say* she shouldn't have allowed him into her heart; it was another thing completely to keep him out. And because of the nature of the man he was, she knew that getting over him was going to be an impossibility.

She gave a guilty start as a knock sounded on the door, staring at it like a startled doe.

It had to be David, he had to have come back for some reason, she realised in dismay, brushing hurriedly at the tears that still dampened her cheeks. She couldn't allow him to see her like that, wasn't up to answering the questions that would engender.

The two men standing outside in the driving snow didn't need blue uniforms to proclaim their profession, the casual clothes and heavy winter coats doing nothing to disguise the fact that they were policemen.

Jade recoiled as if she had been struck, caught completely unawares. And then she admonished herself for showing such a reaction; she had been expecting them for some time, after all. In fact, she was surprised they had taken this long to come and talk to her.

She faced them with calm dignity now that she had herself under control again. 'Please come in, gentlemen,' she invited stiffly.

'Miss Roberts, we're——'

'I know who you are,' she calmly interrupted the older of the two men as he seemed determined they should introduce themselves in their official capacity. Who else but policemen would know her real name in this vicinity?

'Detective-Inspector Shelton, and Detective-Sergeant James,' the man continued as if she hadn't spoken, although the younger man looked a little uncomfortable about the intrusion, a fact he quickly disguised as he saw she was looking at him.

'I hope we haven't interrupted anything.' He looked pointedly at the television set as it still continued to play, the sound not too intrusive, although it was noticeable.

Detective-Inspector Shelton made a point of looking at the watch on his wrist. 'Been watching the news, have you, Miss Roberts?' Grey-blue eyes pinned her to the spot. 'It *is* Miss Roberts, isn't it?'

He was good, Jade realised abstractedly, knowing he meant to unnerve her. But she was used to experts, had learnt to distance herself from the pressure they could exert while seeming to be polite. 'Why don't you just get to the point of your visit?' She moved impatiently to switch off the television set.

'Unless you would prefer us to use the name Mellors——'

'I'm sure none of us has any time to waste,' she prompted waspishly, wishing she had on something more substantial than her robe for this confrontation, all the more defensive because she felt at such a disadvantage dressed like this.

Grey brows rose over those hard grey-blue eyes, iron-grey hair brushed rigidly back from his face, deep lines grooved beside his pale features, as if the life he lived had totally disillusioned him more than once. And in the profession he had chosen to pursue, maybe that wasn't so surprising. 'I'm sure none of us has, Miss Roberts,' he drawled. 'But we didn't like to announce our presence before this.'

Jade looked at him blankly for several seconds, and then, as his meaning became clear, humiliated colour darkened her cheeks, pain clouding her eyes. They had been watching from a distance all the time David was here, had—had—— Oh, God!

'We thought it might make things less awkward for you if we waited until after your—guest had left,' the younger man explained quietly.

She sat down heavily in an armchair, all pretence of self-confidence gone. And not even the fact that these two men had probably desired just this result made any difference to the way she now felt; David had seemed like a beauty completely separate from this part of her life, and now even that time with him had been made to seem as ugly as the rest of it.

'You will have realised that Peter Gifford has escaped from prison?' Detective-Inspector Shelton prompted with husky intent.

That was right, hit her when she was already down. But then, wasn't that just the way they were trained to carry out these sort of investigations? Jade acknowledged with dull pain.

'Has Gifford been in touch with you, Miss Roberts?' Once again the younger man was gentle with her, but Jade distrusted even that, knowing it was another part of the routine, one man tough, the other seeming more approachable and sympathetic.

'Been in touch with me?' she repeated incredulously. 'Been in touch with me?' she said again, more shrilly this time. 'I've spent the majority of the last eighteen months trying to forget I ever knew the man; why should he be in touch with *me*?'

The older man held up his hands defensively. 'Miss Roberts, we're just making enquiries——'

She stood up forcefully, her eyes blazing, her hands twisted painfully together. 'I was subjected to the same sort of "enquiries" eighteen months ago,' she snapped tautly. 'And unless you have some charges you wish to make against me, I suggest you——'

'Miss Roberts, please believe me when I say we have no intention——'

'If some of our colleagues were a little—heavy-handed, in the past then I apologise,' the older man cut in with slow emphasis. 'But these investigations are completely separate from those, and we——'

'Do you, or do you not, have any charges you wish to make against me?' she insisted through clenched teeth, so tense she felt as if she might snap with the strain of it.

'Of course we have no charges to make,' Detective-Inspector Shelton said impatiently. 'We're just making routine enquiries, and as you were once involved with Gifford we naturally——'

'Naturally,' she cut in sarcastically. 'But I have no intention of "helping the police with their enquiries",' she bit out harshly. 'Now, if you have nothing further to say,' she wrenched the door open, standing rigidly beside it as the snow blew inside in gusts, 'I would like you to leave.'

The younger man looked at her sympathetically. 'We understand this is difficult for you, Miss Roberts, but we have a job to do——'

'I doubt you understand the first thing about how I feel,' she choked scornfully. How could these two men possibly understand?

Detective-Inspector Shelton gave a heavy sigh. 'We're sorry to have bothered you, Miss Roberts.'

The blaze in her eyes told him exactly what he could do with his perfunctory apology.

'We realise you're upset, Miss Roberts, but if you should happen to hear from Gifford——' He broke off uncomfortably as the blaze in her eyes became a fierce fire.

'I won't!' Jade rasped as the two men reached the door, daring him to dispute the claim with the proud lift of her chin.

The older man shook his head. 'I wish you would realise that we're only trying to help——'

'The best way you can help *me* is to leave!' she grated forcefully.

He sighed. 'You have our names if you should change your mind——'

'I won't change my mind because I won't hear from Peter.' She was shaking with her anger, staring rigidly at the wall opposite as first one policeman left and then the other, the latter, Detective-Sergeant James, giving a regretful shake of his head as he passed.

Jade closed the door with controlled movements behind them, the gusting wind outside muffling the sound of their departing vehicle, but she did hear them leave, and relaxed with shaky relief.

Not only had those men brought the past back into sharp focus, but they had also managed, in the last few minutes, to degrade something that had been so beautiful to her. Not with what they had said particularly, but with what they *hadn't* said.

The nightmare of having once loved Peter Gifford just went on and on and on...

CHAPTER EIGHT

THERE was no soft thud of snow on the window-
pane to wake her up this morning, no gentle
laughter with David in the snow, with them both
soaking wet, but happy and relaxed together. There
wasn't even a gentle awakening, with Wellington
stretching lazily at her side as he started his day;
the hammering below on the door had caused him
to leap off the bed with an indignant yowl, digging
his claws into Jade's thigh as he leapt across her.

Which was why she had awoken with such a sick-
ening start of surprise.

The clock beside the bed told her it was almost
nine o'clock, late by her standards, but she had had
such a restless night's sleep that her lids felt like
sandpaper rasping across her eyes as she moved
them up and down to clear her vision.

And she didn't want to go downstairs and face
whoever it was on the other side of that door.

She didn't want to face anyone ever again. In
fact, if she could have done, she would have left
last night without having to see David again, but
the falling snow had made her departure impossible. And now it seemed she wasn't to make
her escape today without at least one confrontation.

The pounding on the door grew louder, more in-
sistent, and she knew the culprit wasn't about to

be fobbed off by the lack of response so far to that determined knocking.

Wellington was glaring fiercely at the front door when Jade got down the stairs a few seconds later; if it was David—and she couldn't think of anyone else that persistent!—then he was definitely going to be out of favour with the cat again!

The banging came to an abrupt halt as soon as Jade threw back the bolt at the bottom of the door in preparation of turning the key in the lock, and she felt her tension rise as she hesitated about doing the latter, a sick feeling in the pit of her stomach as she just stood there. What if David had realised who she was after all the renewed publicity in the media about Peter? What if——

'Jade, open this door,' she was told firmly, the voice definitely female.

Jade dazedly did as she was told, her fingers fumbling slightly with the key.

'Jade, thank God!' The woman outside threw herself gratefully into her arms.

Jade was still so stunned that she couldn't think straight, and then the relief at the identity of her visitor washed over her, filled with a choking exhilaration. 'Cathy!' She tightly returned the other woman's hug. 'Oh, God, Cathy!' The tears began to fall; she was hardly able to believe that her best friend was really here. She had felt so alone until now, so devastatingly alone——

'I know, love. I know.' It wasn't until Cathy answered her that Jade realised she had spoken out loud, Cathy still holding her as she looked down at her compassionately. 'But you aren't alone any more,' she assured her with quiet confidence.

Jade pulled her friend fully inside, closing the door to shut out the icy cold, although the act didn't do anything to dispel the chill inside the cottage. Not that that was important at this moment; she could see by Cathy's expression that the heating—or lack of it—was the last thing on Cathy's mind at the moment too.

Cathy Gilbert was the exact opposite of herself to look at: tall and blonde, with a natural grace and sophistication that even the denims and thick jumper over a blouse couldn't disguise. She looked as if she should be an actress or a fashion model with her beauty, instead of the personal assistant—to one of the most difficult men to work for in the City—that she was in reality.

Jade gave a heavy sigh, pushing back her own untidy locks. 'You heard about Peter?'

'On the news late last night.' Cathy nodded acknowledgment, even her voice sexily attractive. The way that she looked often fooled people into ignoring the fact that she was also a very intelligent woman. At twenty-six she had managed to fend off even the most persistent of male advances, and Jade had a feeling that was because she had more than an inkling of affection for her infuriatingly demanding boss, Dominic Reynolds. 'I came as soon as I heard.'

She gave a rueful smile. 'And Dominic meekly allowed you to do that?'

Grey eyes flashed. 'I didn't ask him, I *told* him I was coming!'

Jade's brows rose; she knew Cathy wasn't in the habit of 'jumping' when Dominic Reynolds said 'jump', but she also knew Cathy didn't openly challenge him either. Usually. 'I haven't caused friction between the two of you, have I?' she winced regretfully.

'No more than there usually is,' her friend dismissed carelessly. 'It won't do Dominic any harm at all to realise that helping one of my friends is more important to me than being his damned personal assistant!'

Jade sensed a hidden story behind the remarks, but she could also tell from the reckless glint in Cathy's eyes that she wasn't yet ready to talk about it. 'He would never be stupid enough to really upset you,' she drawled. 'You're too good at your job.'

'And always too damned available,' Cathy snapped a little bitterly. 'At least, he *assumes* that I am. Damn him.'

There *was* something new, an undercurrent, in Cathy's relationship with Dominic Reynolds that hadn't been there before, and at any other time Jade might have tried to persuade her friend to tell her about it, but she knew by the stubborn set to Cathy's jaw that she wouldn't be successful today, that for the moment Cathy would only discuss Jade's own problem.

And, lord knew, that was bad enough!

'What on earth did Peter have to escape from prison for?' Cathy said crossly.

Jade shrugged. 'He still has quite a lot of his sentence to finish——'

'I didn't mean that quite as literally as it sounded,' her friend said ruefully. 'I just meant, why on earth did he have to *do* something like that?' She scowled, her beauty in no way marred.

Jade had never been able to understand why Dominic Reynolds didn't see and appreciate that beauty, but he seemed to be a man who was completely engrossed in his career, a man who didn't see women as women at all, except as an unnecessary diversion to what was really important to him: his business empire.

'He probably heard that you were finally putting your life back together and wanted to ruin that for you, too!' her friend continued scathingly.

There had never been any love lost between Cathy and Peter, but since Peter's behaviour eighteen months ago Cathy had been openly antagonistic. As Jade had herself!

But she doubted Cathy realised just how much she had been 'putting her life back together', just how much Peter had robbed her of this time. Unless she had already been to the Kendrick house? Spoken to David himself?

She looked at her friend warily. For all that she and Cathy had been friends for years, she had realised from talking to Penny the last few days that Cathy was more than a little fond of David, in a brotherly fashion, of course, Penny had hastily assured her. Cathy might not feel too happy about the possibility of her having hurt him, uninten-tional though it might be.

But Cathy didn't seem angry, not with her, at least.

'He succeeded,' Jade answered dully.

Cathy looked at her sharply. 'You aren't thinking of doing anything silly?'

'Such as?' she prompted flatly.

'Such as leaving here,' her friend said im-patiently. 'You told me you love it here,' she re-minded Jade of what she had written in her letters to her since coming to Devon.

'I do——'

'Then you have no reason to leave now,' Cathy told her firmly.

'Peter is on the loose out there somewhere, and he's already been the cause of two policemen paying me a not-too-friendly visit, and you claim I have no reason to want to leave!' She shook her head in nervous agitation.

'Penny and Simon are well aware of your in-volvement with Peter in the past——'

'But my pupils' parents, unfortunately, aren't,' Jade reminded her with self-derision.

'But——'

'They would probably form a lynch-mob if they did know,' she added bitterly.

Cathy gave an impatient sigh. 'You were never charged with anything——'

'That doesn't alter the fact that I was involved in the thing right up to my neck!' Tears glistened on her lashes. 'No, I'm finished here, Cathy.' She shook her head, knowing she was finished in more ways than one. 'I'm very grateful to Penny and Simon for giving me this chance, but I intend leaving for London as soon as I can make my excuses to them.' She dared not even think about saying goodbye to David. 'I'm sure they will understand in the circumstances.'

'You're running away,' her friend accused.

Her eyes flashed. '*Yes*, I'm running away! As fast as the weather will allow.' She frowned out of the window at the blanket of snow on the ground, for the first time noticing the Audi Quattro in the driveway. 'Yours?' She turned to Cathy.

'Dominic's,' her friend grimaced. 'Once he realised I was serious about coming here he was only too happy to provide my transport.'

At the risk of losing the best personal assistant he had ever had if he didn't, Jade wouldn't be surprised!

'It really is good to see you,' she told Cathy emotionally.

Her friend's expression softened. 'You, too. Although I had thought it would be under different circumstances.' Cathy frowned. 'You can't let him chase you away from here, Jade,' she added pleadingly. 'They will have recaptured him within a few days, and a couple of days after that he will have been forgotten again.' She shook her head. 'He simply isn't worth completely upsetting your life for a second time.'

'I wish I had realised that the *first* time.' Jade gave a derisive laugh that completely lacked amusement. 'But I—oh, no,' she gave a pained groan as an all-too-familiar, silver-coloured Range Rover pulled into the driveway behind the Audi.

She didn't for one moment believe Penny and Simon had broken their confidence to her by talking to David about Peter, and David *had* promised he wouldn't come here today, so what other reason could he have for turning up now? Unless—oh, God, she couldn't bear it if somehow the media had already picked up on her part in Peter's past and had dragged the whole sordid business up once again!

She gave a shudder of distaste as she remembered the horror she had known eighteen months ago when she had seen her own photograph next to Peter's on the front page of the daily newspapers. Of course, she had looked a little different then—about forty pounds heavier in weight, for one thing!—but perhaps she was still recognisable from those photographs to someone who knew her well. And David had come to know her very well in the last few days, intimately so.

'What is it?' Cathy had come to stand at her side, looking out of the window too. 'David!' she cried excitedly, turning to run and open the door to him as he came down the pathway.

'Cath——' But she was too late to stop the other woman running out into the snow to launch herself into David's arms, laughing and talking at the same time as she did so.

David looked initially stunned at being assaulted by a blonde-haired woman he didn't at first recognise, a heavy scowl crossing his features. But, as he realised who his assailant was, his smile was one of open pleasure, his arms closing about Cathy as he swung her around in the snow, much to her obvious delight.

Jade watched them enviously. Oh, not because of the affection that was so apparent between them, she could see that was that of a brother and sister. No, she just wished she felt free enough to show her own pleasure so completely without restraint at seeing him. As it was, she wasn't quite sure what sort of reception she was going to get from David, didn't know yet what he was doing here.

The other couple were walking towards the cottage now, their arms about each other's waists as Cathy chattered excitedly, and David smiled down at her indulgently as he listened.

Jade tensed as they entered the cottage, looking searchingly at David. His enigmatic expression didn't tell her anything at all about his thoughts or feelings, although he did look slightly grim around the eyes.

'David's here,' Cathy announced unnecessarily, unable to take her glowing eyes off him. 'I can't believe it!' She shook her head, obviously overjoyed to see him once again. 'Just as I don't believe there isn't a story behind that black eye,' she added teasingly. 'Although he insists there isn't!'

The fact that she *was* seeing David again after all this time, that he was apparently back among the family, seemed to have blinded Cathy to the most obvious fact of all: David was *here*, at Jade's cottage, and definitely without the knowledge that Cathy would be here. But it was a lack of vision on Cathy's part that Jade was grateful for at this moment. Cathy wouldn't give her any peace at all once she realised she and David had become more than friends since his arrival here, and she hoped to have left the area herself before that happened.

Navy blue eyes looked at Jade compellingly, and she met that gaze guardedly, still uncertain as to the reason David had altered their arrangements and come to see her this morning, after all. Although she was grateful to him for not giving Cathy the details about that black eye.

'Your telephone line is down,' he explained softly as he was easily able to guess her thoughts.

She looked surprised, turning to frown at the offending instrument as it sat so innocently on the table; as if frowning at it was going to do any good! 'I had no idea,' she said weakly, wishing she had at least known that fact so that she could have been half prepared for his arrival, when he hadn't managed to reach her by telephone as he had said he would this morning, instead of being caught completely unawares.

'Unfortunately, so are a lot of others,' he shrugged, very attractive in a dark green jumper and faded denims beneath his leather jacket, 'so I don't think you'll be treated as a priority.'

'It doesn't matter,' she dismissed abruptly. 'Although it was very nice of you to come out and check up on me,' she added awkwardly, more for Cathy's benefit than anything else.

'I thought you had—company—when I first drove up,' he told her, his eyes narrowed.

'And aren't I company?' Cathy pretended indignation, her eyes twinkling mischievously.

'Not the sort I meant,' David drawled.

He had believed, when he saw the Audi outside, that she had had the ulterior motive of another man for not wanting to see him today. And that was the reason he had been scowling when he arrived. It was a relief to know that the past hadn't all blown up in her face. At least, not yet.

Cathy pouted prettily. 'I do think Penny and Simon could have telephoned me to let me know you were here.' She shook her head reprovingly. 'I would have come down here all the sooner if I had known.'

David gave Jade a piercing look before turning his attention to the other woman. 'Maybe they didn't think Dominic could stand the competition,' he teased.

It didn't surprise Jade at all that David should speak of the other man with familiarity; the two men moved in the same business circles.

'There would have been no competition,' Cathy dismissed scathingly. 'As soon as I had heard you were here I would have come down. It's been too long, David,' she added softly, her face full of emotional affection.

'Yes,' he acknowledged gruffly. 'But don't you think you should let Penny and Simon know you are here? Penny was so sure you weren't going to make it again this year either.' He shook his head ruefully. 'The names she's been calling Dominic...! I think I should have a word with him, you know; he's obviously working you much too hard if he can't even give you Christmas off!'

'As bosses go, he's pretty awful,' Cathy conceded.

'But?' David arched dark brows.

She looked at him slightly defensively. 'Is there a but?'

He returned her gaze speculatively. 'I would say so—but that is obviously another story,' he dismissed shruggingly at Cathy's warning glare that he was trespassing on a very touchy subject. 'From the look of Jade, we've both caught her at an inconvenient time.' He lightly drew attention to the fact that she was still wearing her dressing-gown when they were both fully clothed. He turned back to Cathy with a puzzled frown. 'You must have driven most of the night to get here this early; there's nothing wrong, is there?'

'Not at all,' she dismissed breezily, her gaze unwavering in her lie. 'The opportunity came to leave and so I took it!'

'Before Dominic changed his mind,' David drawled understandingly.

'Exactly.' Cathy gave him a companionable grin.

He nodded before turning back to Jade. 'How are you feeling this morning?'

That bogus chill came back to haunt her once again! She wished she had never invented the damned thing.

'I feel fine, thank you,' she answered abruptly. 'Although a nice long soak in a hot bath wouldn't come amiss,' she added pointedly. After all, these two could go off somewhere and reminisce without her. She badly needed the time to do her packing.

'Have you been ill?' Cathy instantly frowned her concern. 'You should have told me——'

'It was only a chill.' Her dismissal was made irritably this time, annoyed that David had drawn attention to yesterday's indisposition—or rather, the lack of it!

'Nevertheless——'

'I have a feeling Jade would rather we changed the subject,' David drawled as her eyes flashed at Cathy's continued concern.

'But—oh, where did you come from?' Cathy enthused as Wellington walked haughtily into the room to see what all the noise was about, going down on her haunches to call to him, gently stroking his silky fur as he deigned to stand in front of her. 'What's your name?' she cooed at the disdainful cat.

'Wellington—for obvious reasons,' David supplied drily at Jade's lack of response.

She had got to the stage where she just wanted them both to leave, something neither of them seemed inclined to do!

'You're beautiful,' Cathy told Wellington admiringly. 'You never mentioned in your letters that you have a cat now,' she lightly scolded Jade, still stroking the silky cat, who now seemed to consider that anyone entering Jade's home had to pass his approval, too! Cathy obviously did.

'He's a stray.' Jade shrugged frowningly, as if that explained her lack of explanation earlier.

'He doesn't look like a stray to me,' her friend admonished teasingly. 'You surely don't intend to leave him behind when you go?' She sounded scandalised at the idea.

'Of course Wellington will go with me, *when* I go,' she muttered the last warningly.

'Well, I should think so.' Cathy took absolutely no notice of the warning, her attention back on the cat as he twirled in and out of her hands for extra cuddles. 'It would never do to leave this beautiful creature behind.'

'No,' Jade grated, frowning darkly, keeping her eyes averted as she sensed David's searching gaze on her.

'All this talk of your leaving,' he spoke slowly. 'Is that imminent?'

Well, Cathy was certainly doing nothing to give the impression it wasn't!

Really, much as she loved Wellington herself, and had no intention of leaving without him, she wished her friend would pay a little less attention to him and a little more to the conversation.

'Cathy was talking about when the permanent teacher returns at the end of the next term,' she explained lightly. Although until yesterday she had half hoped the other woman would decide not to return to work, after all, so she could remain in her place. That was now an impossibility for her.

'Of course,' David nodded, but he looked far from convinced. 'Talking about leaving——' He looked pointedly at Cathy.

'Hm, I suppose we should be on our way.' She straightened, innocently assuming he would be leaving with her now that he had satisfied himself as to Jade's health and safety. 'Actually, it's a lot worse here than it was in London, so I'll be glad of the back-up to Penny and Simon's.' She grimaced. 'Not that I'll ever admit to Dominic how bad the weather has been; he thought I was slightly insane coming down last night in the first place!'

'Only slightly?' David derided drily.

Cathy gave him an affectionate punch on the arm. 'It may be years since I last saw you, but you're still a dreadful tease!'

'And you're still as impulsive as ever,' he mocked. 'You must have wanted to join Penny and Simon very much to have driven down in that storm last night.' There was a question in his tone, his gaze piercing.

'Or else I wanted to get *away* very badly,' Cathy lightly avoided, not committing herself either way. 'Now we had better go so that at least Jade can get dressed in peace and quiet.'

'Hm,' David accepted reluctantly, obviously not satisfied with the arrangement at all. But what else could he do in the circumstances? Jade, by her own behaviour, had made it obvious she had no intention of telling Cathy about their relationship, and he simply wasn't the type of man to openly claim that relationship without the woman's permission;

especially when in the past Jade had made it so apparent that she would rather there *wasn't* a relationship. And her attitude towards him today had given him little encouragement to believe there *was* a relationship between them!

''Bye, love.' Cathy came over to hug her. 'I'll see you soon. And don't you dare leave!' The last was added in a fierce whisper. 'We still have so much catching up to do,' she added loudly as she stepped back.

Jade searched her friend's face for any hidden meaning behind those words, wondering if Cathy had picked up on that tangible 'something' that there was between David and herself, after all. But Cathy just looked very stern, daring her to go before they had spoken again.

'I'll call for you at about eight this evening,' David told her quietly but firmly.

'The party may be cancelled if the weather doesn't improve,' she dismissed.

He shook his head. 'Even if it's only the five of us there, plus the children, Penny will want to throw a party for the arrival of her little sister.'

'Not so little,' Cathy grinned.

'I can see that,' he teased, receiving another punch on the arm for his trouble.

Jade sighed, more or less sure in her own mind that she wouldn't be here by this evening. But she nodded non-committally. 'I'll give Penny and Simon a ring as soon as my telephone has been reconnected.'

She stood at the door as the other couple left, coming back inside as the icy cold wind pierced her brief clothing. But mainly she just didn't want to watch David drive away from her, probably out of her life completely.

She turned around sharply as the cottage door opened quietly behind her, unable to stop her cry of joy as she saw it was David returned. Just as she was unable to stop herself running into his waiting arms...

'I know you didn't want to see me today,' he spoke warmly into the thickness of her hair. 'But when I discovered your telephone was out of action I was worried about you. Don't be angry with me for being concerned, Jade,' he groaned.

How could she be angry with him? She loved him, knew it beyond a single doubt.

'Jade?' He looked down at her pleadingly, his eyes dark with the same emotion as was in her heart.

'I'm not angry with you.' She shook her head, gazing up at him. 'Kiss me. And then you'll have to go, before Cathy becomes curious about your delay and decides to investigate.'

His mouth twisted. 'I told her I'd forgotten to relate some message from Penny. God, I missed being with you last night!' he added raggedly. 'Jade—oh God, Jade, I——'

Her fingertips over his lips stopped further talk; she couldn't bear to actually hear his emotions put into words. Because they too closely resembled her own. And there was no future for them together.

Only now. This moment. And she put all of the depth of her feelings into the kiss they shared, clinging to him unashamedly as their lips parted and they just held each other, neither needing anything else but that closeness for the moment.

'If only Cathy weren't outside,' David shakily murmured his longing.

'But she is,' Jade smiled gently. 'Drive back carefully.' My darling, she didn't add, but wished she dared. For he was. Her darling. In a matter of days he had become the most important part of her life. In a matter of days? More like a matter of minutes! For that was all the time it had taken, she felt sure, for David to find his way into her heart.

He looked down at her darkly. 'Let me stay with you when I bring you back tonight?'

Tonight...

'Yes,' she agreed breathlessly, knowing it was a promise she would never keep. Because by tonight she would have gone.

The apartment looked more unwelcoming than usual, just four walls that succeeded in assuring her privacy, with no fire burning warmly in the hearth, because there wasn't a fireplace. Oh, the flat was comfortable enough, with its central heating, but it lacked any real warmth.

Wellington definitely wasn't impressed with it, just as he wasn't impressed with the fact that he couldn't go outside to investigate his surroundings, totally disgusted with the cat-tray she had managed to provide for him.

'It won't be for long, boy,' Jade assured him distractedly. 'Just until I can find somewhere more comfortable.'

His expression of disgust didn't change, and Jade knew she was going to have more than a little trouble with him in the near future.

Not that any of today had been easy, least of all finding a hire-car company that could provide her with a four-wheel-drive vehicle at such short notice. She had only managed to do so in the end because the company had received a cancellation from someone who had considered the road conditions too unsafe to drive on even in such a heavy vehicle. She had had to leave poor Cleo at a local garage, promising to collect her when the weather cleared if they would service her for her. Not that the car needed servicing, but it had given her a legitimate excuse to ask them to hold on to it for her.

So here she was, back in London, in a flat that seemed more lonely than it usually did, and even this was only a temporary stop, any further escape limited because of Wellington's presence. But, as Cathy had pointed out, she couldn't even think about not bringing the cat with her. As soon as she could find somewhere else, out of London preferably, for them to stay, they would be moving on.

When the knock first sounded on the door she thought there had to be some sort of mistake; she had been away from the flat for months, so who on earth could be calling on her tonight of all nights? She knew very few people in London anyway, certainly no one who could know she was back here——

'Open this door, Jade, I know damn well you're in there,' Cathy suddenly called angrily through the door.

Cathy. She should have known her friend wouldn't let the situation rest with her departure. What did she do now? If she refused to acknowledge her, she didn't doubt for a moment that Cathy would persist until she did. But she simply wasn't sure she was up to the verbal chastisement if she did open the door.

'Wellington's pleased to hear me, even if you aren't,' Cathy pointed out drily.

The silly cat was meowing at the door as if he had found a long-lost friend! And maybe he thought he had; Cathy had certainly been present when he was in that other, more comfortable world, at the cottage. A life he obviously wanted to return to.

Cathy marched straight by her into the flat once Jade had unlocked the door for her, her grey eyes blazing. 'How could you?' she attacked furiously. 'How could you just up and leave like that? Poor David is devastated. And don't try to deny that the poor man's in love with you, because we both know that he is. God, I must have been so blind not to have seen that this morning,' she said self-disgustedly. 'But little old innocent me accepted completely that he had driven over because Pen and Simon were worried about you—until David fell apart when he got to the cottage and found you had packed up and left! That was cruel, Jade, so damned cruel.' She shook her head disappointedly.

'*That* was cruel?' she echoed shakily, knowing how devastated she had been by *having* to pack up and leave, feeling that wrenching pain again as she heard about David's heartache. 'How much crueller would it have been to have stayed and involved him in the mess I've made of my life?'

'You didn't make it——'

'Does it really matter who made it so?' Jade said wearily. 'The facts are that it is.'

'You could try telling David the truth,' Cathy challenged. 'He would have understood, I'm sure of it. Penny says he's in love with you—if I needed any additional proof after he got back from the cottage,' she said raggedly.

Yes, she knew David was in love with her now, as she was in love with him, but how long would that love survive, how long after he was told the truth would he begin to have doubts and believe what the police, her family, and almost everyone else in the country had believed so easily eighteen months ago—that she had been involved with Peter in the Marshall kidnapping, in the abduction of a defenceless five-year-old girl for the money they would receive in exchange for her release...?

CHAPTER NINE

IT HADN'T been true, of course, none of it. But, despite the fact that she had never been officially charged with the crime, she had always felt guilty. The evidence against her had been so great...

She was Selina Marshall's form teacher, one of the five teachers in charge of the pupils that day they went to the beach on a trip, she was engaged to marry the man who had eventually been proven to have planned the crime, had even, unwittingly though it may have been, provided Peter with all the details of their movements that day, having believed he was taking an interest for her sake.

She had been a fool ever to believe Peter's interest in her was genuine, had often wondered at her luck in attracting such a handsome man when she was so obviously overweight, wore heavy-rimmed glasses, and had hair such a deep shade of red that she tried to keep it hidden as much as possible by pulling it back in a bun at her nape. It had even been summer when they'd met, and she had been covered in freckles! But Peter had assured her he found everything about her delightful, even the freckles.

She still cringed at how gullible she had been: an overripe plum ripe for the picking—or in this case, fooling!

With hindsight, she was able to see that even that very first meeting between them had been engineered by Peter when he 'accidentally' gave Cleo a gentle knock on the bumper which necessitated an exchange of addresses. Even then Peter hadn't rushed things, simply making sure the minor damage to Cleo was repaired. Then they had met in town one day, another 'accident', Jade had thought, as they fell easily into conversation, shyly accepting when he had offered to buy her a cup of coffee. That had been the beginning of the relationship that had shattered her life.

She had been a fool, and that was the only crime she had really been guilty of, and Peter, with his handsome, blond-haired, blue-eyed good looks, had known exactly how to flatter her and convince her that he found her utterly irresistible.

How could she have guessed that he had an ulterior motive for becoming close to her, that it was imperative to his plans that he gain the confidence of Selina Marshall's teacher? God, she could have been a sixty-year-old spinster, and his plans would still have been the same!

As it was, Jade had been flattered by Peter's interest, had accepted when the coffee together led to a dinner invitation.

It had been the first of many dates they had had, and for over two months Jade had lived in a euphoria of believing her love was returned. They had even become engaged, her ring of tiny diamonds surrounding an emerald that Peter claimed matched the colour of her eyes.

How could she have known, how could she have even guessed, that it was all because Peter was looking for a chink in the security that always surrounded all of the Marshall family, but their only child in particular?

And she had unknowingly provided him with that chink, had blithely told him of the visit of the lower three classes at the school to the beach for the day, giving him the opening he had so patiently waited for.

Even once Peter and his associates had Selina he hadn't left Jade's life, had even been the one to comfort her during the next two days while the kidnappers made their demands and waited for them to be met. He wasn't taking any chances on not being completely informed, and he knew, because of her love for him, that Jade had every reason to confide in him!

The only thing she could say to his credit was that Selina had been returned to her parents once the ransom money had been paid over, physically unharmed, at least. Mentally it was another matter, the little girl suffering with nightmares, giving every reason to suppose that she would suffer the mental torment of what had happened to her for the rest of her life.

And still Peter had stayed on. To do anything else would have looked too suspicious. His idea had been to break their engagement and disappear from her life after a decent interval had elapsed since the kidnapping.

So he had stayed on, helping Jade through the trauma of what had happened to one of her pupils, discussing wedding plans with her just as if he actually intended to go through with the spring wedding.

She had received the shock of her life when the police began to requestion her before moving on to Peter. They had claimed it was 'routine', but they kept coming back again and again, until finally Peter had cracked under the strain and tried to get away from the country with the ransom money.

In the midst of the pained shock of realising the man she loved had committed such a heinous crime, Jade had had to stand by while he told her—and the rest of the world!—that she had merely been a means to an end, a gullible convenience he hadn't hesitated in exploiting.

In the eyes of the law his testimony had cleared her of any guilt, but in the eyes of the general public it had been something else entirely. The fact that Peter had stood in a court of law and denounced her for the simple fool she had been didn't mean anything to them, and Jade had had to face their stares and speculation. No one had asked for her resignation, but she had tendered it just the same, knowing she had become an embarrassment to all concerned.

Her family had stood by her through it all, and she had turned to them as her salvation once she didn't even have a job, moving back home with her parents. Until she realised that her parents had stopped going out to see friends, and that no one came to see them at the house either. When her father had his heart attack she had known she had to leave, that she was as responsible for that as much as she was for Peter's success in kidnapping Selina. And so she had left her parents' house, and she hadn't told them where she was going, either, sure they would be able to put their lives back together if they no longer had her for a daughter. Maybe it was self-pity that made her do such a thing, but she just hadn't known what else to do.

For over a year she had lived alone in London, surviving off the money she had managed to save in the years before she left her job, Cathy her only visitor; she had not even bothered to look for other employment, even though there was nothing except her own guilty feelings to stop her from doing so. She felt too sickened with herself, with her stupidity, to face the outside world again.

It had been Cathy who had finally pushed her out to face that world, arranging for the temporary job at Simon and Penny's school, the other couple also of the opinion that she didn't have to suffer for the rest of her life when she was completely innocent of doing anything wrong except for falling in love with the wrong man.

And now she was in love with the right man, a gentle, beautiful man, who she wouldn't drag back down with her. Because she *was* about to go down again, would never be free of Peter and the guilt he had brought into her life.

'Yes, perhaps you're right and he would understand,' she answered Cathy bitterly. 'But he's already known so much unhappiness in his life; I have no intention of adding to it.'

'You make him happy,' her friend protested. 'Penny told me all about the way you first met, about his claim that he's going to marry you——'

'None of that matters now, Cathy.' She shook her head, doing all that she could to block the memories from her mind. 'David loves children, would make a wonderful father himself; how could he ever accept the pain I unwittingly caused an innocent child?'

'The key word in that statement is "unwittingly",' Cathy pointed out firmly. 'You had no idea what was going on. Anyone who really knows you would realise that.'

Her parents had 'really known her', and yet, before she left, before her father had his heart attack, she had sensed them watching her whenever they thought she wasn't aware of it, had felt their doubts. And they had known and loved her all her life, so what chance did David have of coming through what had happened in her past with his feelings unscathed? She couldn't bear to see that disillusionment in his eyes.

'Possibly,' she answered non-committally. 'But the doubt would always be there, festering, growing, until it utterly destroyed the love.' She knew; hadn't she watched it happen with her own parents? They loved her, she had never doubted that, but even they couldn't help the doubt that had crept in unwanted... 'How happy would I make him then, Cathy?' she said harshly, knowing she had to be strong now for both David's and her own sake. She just had to!

'You're underestimating him, Jade——'

'No, I'm trying to protect him!' she defended fiercely, her eyes dark.

'Oh, Jade.' Cathy's face was full of compassion. 'You love him so much, too.'

'I——' She broke off, shaking her head against the denial she had been about to make. 'Yes, I love him,' she admitted in a controlled voice. 'And no one can take that away from me.'

'Oh, love.' Cathy's arms came about her to hug her tightly.

Jade's control shattered, the tight hold she had maintained over her emotions since leaving Devon this morning completely gone as she sobbed out her utter despair.

'What a pair we are,' Cathy finally choked self-derisively, her own cheeks wet as she stepped back slightly. 'Oh, Jade——' she shook her head '—what are we going to do with you?'

'Is this a private cry-in, or can anyone join in?' an all-too-familiar voice murmured.

Both women spun around, Cathy in surprise, Jade guiltily. She couldn't really claim to be surprised to see David again, hadn't for a moment believed he would accept her departure and telephone call to Penny and Simon as final to their relationship. She just hadn't expected to see him again as soon as this, that was all!

That he didn't look well was her first thought as she drank in the sight of him. That sparkle of the pure enjoyment of life that had been in his eyes since the moment they met had gone, and in its place was an aching pain, his face haggard and drawn. Of course his strained appearance could just have been due to the fact that he had been driving for several hours in bad conditions—and yet Jade knew that it wasn't. She was the one that had done this to him, had given love back into his life only to rip it away again.

'I did knock, but no one answered,' he explained gruffly, a defeated hunch to his shoulders in the thick sheepskin jacket.

Cathy looked awkwardly between the two of them. 'I think I'll go and make us all a nice cup of tea,' she hastily excused herself.

The silence crackled with tension once Cathy had made her hurried exit to the kitchen.

Jade felt herself shrinking back at the pained re-crimination in David's eyes, swallowing with difficulty, moistening her lips nervously, waiting for his words of reproach, bracing herself for them.

'Do you mind if I take my coat off?'

She gave a visible start; it had been the last thing she expected him to say, despite the heat in the flat.

His mouth twisted. 'It's only my jacket, Jade,' he taunted softly.

Colour warmed her cheeks. 'Please,' she invited abruptly, inwardly wondering if he was going to be here long enough to merit removing the jacket.

He shrugged out of the thick garment, laying it across the back of one of the armchairs with measured movements.

Jade's tension grew. Why didn't he just come right out with it and demand to know what she thought she was doing leaving Devon so abruptly? Why was he standing there so calmly, looking for all the world as if he had just casually dropped in for a visit?

It was certainly obvious to Jade, from the lack of noise coming from the kitchen, that Cathy had no intention of making them some tea, that she intended leaving them to it, would stay out of the way in the kitchen for as long as it took them to have their conversation.

'Nice flat.' David nodded appreciatively.

It was an awful flat, just four walls that had no character to them. 'David——'

'Have you lived here long?' he continued politely, just as if she hadn't spoken in that aching voice.

'About a year,' she dismissed impatiently. 'David, please—— '

'You kept it on even after your move to Devon?' He sounded surprised.

'The job at the school was only a temporary one.' Which was the only reason she had allowed Cathy to persuade her to do it in the first place! 'And flats in London aren't that easy to come by.' She shrugged, frowning deeply. 'David, I'm sure you didn't come here to discuss the merits of my flat.'

'Why not?' he shrugged. 'It's strange really, on the drive up here my mind was whirling with the things I was going to say to you, but now that I'm here none of those things seem to apply.' He gave a deep sigh. 'Why did you leave? What difference does it really make, when you did leave,' he answered his own question. 'You had your reasons for going, and from the wary expression in your eyes—eyes I obviously forgot to "watch",' he added self-derisively, 'you don't feel any more disposed to discussing those reasons with me now than you did this morning!'

'No,' she admitted dully, blinking back the fresh tears that clouded her vision.

He gave a regretful grimace. 'Sure?'

Of course she wasn't sure. She would give anything to be able to tell him the truth and have him tell her everything was going to be all right. But it wasn't, and it wouldn't be, and she wasn't about to hurt him any more than she already had by involving him any further.

'Very,' she told him firmly.

David sighed. 'There doesn't seem a lot more to say, does there?'

Not when your heart was breaking. And hers was shattered, fragmented. 'I wish you hadn't come here, David,' she said huskily.

He gave a harsh laugh, moving an agitated hand through his already tousled dark hair. 'It would be so easy to say I wish I hadn't, too—but it wouldn't be true. You may have decided you don't want me after all, but I'm glad I had this chance to see you again. I'm just sorry I hounded you so much that you felt you had to leave.' He shook his head. 'As soon as Cathy told us where she was going, and why, I realised I had forced you into leaving. I know

now that it wouldn't have mattered how much time I had given you, that time alone doesn't produce love. You tried to tell me, but I didn't want to listen,' he said sadly. 'I came here to tell you that you have no reason not to return to Devon. I don't intend going back myself.'

'Oh, but that's ridiculous,' she protested heatedly. 'You have no reason to leave, and Penny and Simon were so thrilled to see you again.' She frowned. 'I— what if I were to tell you that—you didn't really have anything to do with my leaving?' For the main part that was true; it was Peter's escape that had meant she had to move on. And if it weren't for Peter she could have allowed the beauty of David's love into her life.

David drew in a shuddering breath. 'I would say that if you were hoping to make me feel better you didn't succeed; I feel as if someone just punched me in the stomach while I was standing under a cold shower!'

'I'm sorry,' Jade choked.

He made a rueful face. 'You can't force love.'

'No woman in her right mind could help but love you!' she said intensely.

His mouth twisted. 'You happen to be talking about the woman I want to marry.'

'I wish I could—oh, David,' she quivered emotionally, 'what are we going to do?' Her hands twisted together in her deep agitation.

'*We* aren't going to do anything,' he told her gently, lightly clasping the tops of her arms before tilting her chin up so that she had to look at him.

'*You're* going to return to Devon, to your work at the school, and forget you ever met a delinquent Father Christmas!'

Forget she had met him, when he was the most wonderful thing that had ever happened to her? She would never forget him; it was impossible to forget the man she loved.

Just as she must *never* forget the man she had thought she loved, the man who had fooled her into believing he loved her in return when all he wanted to do was use her for his own ends. It was that misplaced love in her past that had forged her future; a long, lonely existence.

'I never stood a chance of making you forget him, did I, Jade?' David sighed defeatedly.

'Him?' she repeated sharply, her expression one of alarm.

He nodded abruptly. 'The man in your past, the one you can't forget.'

She swallowed hard, her stomach churning. 'What do you know about him?' Her voice was a pained squeak, her throat suddenly dry.

'That he existed,' David said self-derisively. 'It seems to be enough that he did.'

Jade frowned. 'I'm not sure I understand...?'

He shrugged, sighing heavily. 'I loved Sara, I'll never forget her or the love we shared because it meant too much to me to ever do that, but I've learnt to let go. You haven't let go,' he explained simply.

'Because I can't. I can't!' She shook her head in desperate denial. 'You're the one who doesn't understand,' she groaned, tears glistening in her eyes.

'Because I can't,' he said dully. 'I—hello, boy,' he greeted Wellington lightly as he came into the room, going down on his haunches as the snowy white head rubbed against him. 'Not what you're used to, is it, boy?' he sympathised with the cat's obvious distaste for his new surroundings.

'We won't be staying here,' Jade told him defensively, standing tensely across the room from him and the purring cat now.

David looked up at her piercingly. 'No, I don't suppose you will,' he accepted heavily, straightening to shrug his shoulders back into his coat. 'Be happy, wherever you go. I'd better go now.' He sighed his reluctance with that idea.

'I—will you go back to Devon?' she asked unhappily.

He shrugged. 'There's no reason for me not to now, is there?'

She knew he meant her own decision not to go back. 'No,' she answered flatly.

Dark blue eyes roamed hungrily over her face. 'I do want you to be happy, Jade,' he said finally. 'And if you ever do think of that delinquent Father Christmas who wanted more than anything else to be the gift in your bed on Christmas morning—— Forget it,' he dismissed wearily. 'Why should you think of me?' he said wryly. 'Take care, my darling,' he told her softly.

'David——'

'I'll just go and say goodbye to Cathy.' He turned away abruptly.

Jade ached, ached with needing him, with resisting that need.

The closing of the apartment door behind him a few seconds later was like a shot being fired—into her heart!

But she had no time to reflect on her pain as Cathy rushed out of the kitchen, her anger obvious from the fury on her face, her hands clenched fiercely at her sides.

'How could you?' her friend accused heatedly. 'How could you?'

Jade was completely taken aback by the attack. 'I don't——'

'You let David go away from here with the impression that you're still in love with Peter,' Cathy stormed.

'I did no such thing,' she gasped.

'Of course you did,' Cathy disputed disgustedly. 'What else do you think he was talking about when he said you can't forget Peter? And don't tell me I shouldn't have been listening to your conversation,' she warned fiercely. 'The walls are made of papier-mâché, and I was only in the kitchen!'

She hadn't been about to rebuke the other woman, was too disturbed by the other things she had said. Had she let David think she was still in love with Peter, the man in her past? Perhaps, but she couldn't tell him the truth about that time, so it was better that he think she was in love with someone else. 'What difference does it make if he did think that?' she said dismissively. 'Whatever he thinks, there's no future for us.'

'Because you've decided there isn't,' Cathy told her impatiently. 'You're my best friend, Jade, but I have to tell you now that this self-pity can't go on——'

'It isn't self-pity——'

'Of course it is,' her friend dismissed scathingly. 'OK, so Peter played a dirty trick on you, and a lot of people suffered because of it, but no one expects you to keep on suffering for ever. David loves you, and I'm more convinced than ever that you love him; the two of you should be together.'

'It isn't as simple as that——'

'Nothing in life ever is,' Cathy scorned. 'A fact I intend pointing out to Dominic when I give him my resignation.'

'Cathy?' she gasped. 'What——'

'Let's not get sidetracked,' she was told fiercely. 'David loves you, and you love him; you should be able to work out the rest of it. Even Peter,' she put in firmly as Jade would have protested again. 'Tell David the truth and let him decide for himself what was or wasn't true, but for God's sake don't give in without even giving him that chance,' she said disgustedly.

'I'm afraid...' Jade trembled at the thought of being so totally vulnerable.

'Do you think I don't know that?' Cathy groaned sympathetically. 'Of course you're afraid, but that's part of being alive. You've merely been existing this last year, Jade. Do you really want to live in the shadows all your life, or are you willing to take the risk of loving and being loved? It's either that or returning to what it's been like the last year; is that what you want?'

To go back to the emptiness. The loneliness. The nothingness.

Was that really what she wanted?

CHAPTER TEN

THANK God the snow had stopped falling now, although even without that the going was tough.

To Devon.

To David...

Cathy was right, she knew that, knew that however much she feared David's rejection when he knew the truth about her, she had to at least try to come out of the shadows. Just those few hours at her apartment had shown her how lonely her life was going to be again, and even though she had only known David a few days, with him she was alive, truly alive. And those shadows would still be there waiting for her if David didn't want her.

And so she was going back to Devon. Wellington was totally confused at again being bundled into the travelling basket she had so hastily purchased this morning, and the hire company she had got the vehicle from found it a little strange that she wanted to return it to their local office in Devon, after all.

But none of that mattered when David would be waiting at the other end of her journey. Even if it was only briefly, he had to know she loved him in return, probably had since the first moment his dark blue eyes had looked at her so mischievously.

Nevertheless, her body ached with the tension of the drive, and her eyes felt sore from the intense concentration when she at last drove back into the village later that evening. It had been dark for several hours, making driving doubly difficult on the icy, unfamiliar roads, and she just wanted to find David, say her piece, and then know either the ecstasy of his love or the return to those grey shadows that had been her life for the last year.

Penny opened the door to her ring on the doorbell, a Penny whose eyes widened incredulously at the sight of her, her black cocktail dress indicating that she had been expecting quite another sort of guest. 'What——? We thought you were in London,' she gasped, her statement so obviously incorrect as Jade now stood before her.

Jade's mouth twisted. 'I needed to talk to David rather urgently.' She gave a rueful shrug.

The other woman looked puzzled. 'Oh, but— come inside,' she instructed distractedly, opening the door wider to usher Jade into the hallway, opening the door to the dining-room. 'I'm just taking Jade into the sitting-room,' she informed Simon. 'Yes, I said Jade,' she answered his surprised exclamation. 'If anyone arrives for the party just bring them in here and tell them I've been delayed. Or something,' she dismissed impatiently.

'Penny, there's really no need,' Jade protested as the other woman turned in the direction of the sitting-room; in truth she had forgotten all about the party Penny and Simon were having this evening. 'If I could just quickly talk to David——'

'He isn't here,' Penny told her quietly.

Jade's face fell. 'Oh,' she sighed heavily. 'But he said he was coming back here,' she frowned, a sudden pain behind her eyes.

'Perhaps he is,' the other woman shrugged, closing the door behind them. 'But we haven't heard from him since he telephoned to let us know he had arrived safely in London.'

Jade sat down defeatedly in an armchair. 'He said he was coming back here,' she repeated dully, hardly able to believe she had made that horrendous journey only to learn David wasn't here after all.

'Then he probably will,' Penny assured her gently, bending down in front of her. 'Is it going to be all right between you two?' she probed softly.

Jade drew in a shuddering breath, her disappointment extreme at not finding David here when she had so desperately needed to talk to him. If she wasn't able to talk to him now she might never have the nerve or courage to try again.

'Jade?' Penny prompted.

She shook her head. 'I don't know. I thought— I hoped that if I could just talk to him, tell him about——' She broke off, swallowing hard.

'Peter,' the other woman finished with feeling. 'He's been recaptured, you know,' she added softly.

She had heard the announcement on the radio news, but it had meant little to her when his escape had totally disrupted her life a second time! The fact that he was now back behind lock and key where he belonged left her cold, his recapture making little difference to her life, except the relief of knowing he was once again being punished for his crime.

Jade frowned as the doorbell rang. 'I really mustn't keep you from your guests...'

Penny straightened. 'Maybe it's David.' But they both knew it wasn't as Simon could be heard talking jovially before closing the dining-room door behind himself and the new arrival. 'Join the party as originally planned,' Penny invited softly. 'Then if David—then stay the night, at least,' she insisted as Jade fiercely shook her head at her other suggestion. 'It's too late at night to go back to your cold cottage.'

She had to admit the prospect didn't seem very inviting. 'There's Wellington, too,' she grimaced.

The other woman smiled. 'I don't mind, if he doesn't!'

On the few occasions Penny had called at the cottage in the past Wellington had lost no time in letting her know it was his home, and he was to be treated with respect! Jade had no doubt in her mind that Wellington wouldn't distinguish between the two establishments; he had lost no time earlier in letting her know who was boss at her apartment.

'If you're sure you wouldn't mind...?' She frowned. 'I'm really not in the mood for a party.'

'Of course you aren't,' Penny dismissed briskly. 'I'll take you upstairs and see you settled into a room, and then when David returns——'

'*If* he returns,' she corrected heavily; his not being here when she arrived was something she hadn't even considered.

'He told you he was coming back, and so he will,' Penny told her firmly, leading the way up the wide staircase. 'David is a man of his word.'

The last was said a little defensively, Penny obviously wondering how she dared question David's loyalty and trustworthiness. Not that Jade could blame her for feeling a little indignant; there was no comparison between the two men.

It was a lovely, sunny-looking room, decorated in gold and creams, that Penny showed her into, explaining that she would have to share the bathroom with the two boys, their bedrooms just across the hallway. 'They'll be coming up to bed shortly,' Penny dismissed. 'They only stayed up to say hello to everyone. They're getting so excited about Christmas now,' she added affectionately.

Jade had forgotten all about it! The day after tomorrow would be Christmas Day, and she wasn't prepared for it at all. By that time she would either have everything, or nothing, to celebrate...

She was right about Wellington's reaction to his new surroundings: he wasn't at all impressed, although he curled up and went to sleep on the foot of the bed quite amiably once he realised they were staying put for the night.

Jade lay awake in the darkness; she could hear the muted sounds of the party below, heard Penny putting the two boys to bed a little later, and then she was aware of nothing else, the exhaustion of the day taking its toll on her.

She was dreaming of the eyes again, everywhere she looked, accusing eyes. And this time, hard as she searched, she couldn't find that warmly caressing navy blue pair. She looked and looked, but as those navy blue depths remained elusive her panic began to grow.

'Where are you?' she muttered. 'You have to be there. You have to be!' she groaned. 'Oh, David, David, where are you?' she cried, still searching, searching.

'I'm here. I *am* here,' that comforting voice assured firmly as she continued to thrash about wildly.

But she still couldn't find him in that sea of eyes, moving restlessly, whimpering softly.

'Jade! Darling, wake up,' that voice prompted tensely. 'Jade, you have to open your eyes.'

She struggled through the layers of sleep, searching for that voice, but the accusing eyes wanted to hold her back, keep her down in the shadows with them. And she wasn't going to stay, was determined to leave that behind, wanted to be out in the light. With David. And he was waiting for her out there, she knew he was.

'Darling.' She was shaken gently. 'Open your eyes and look at me.'

She trusted him, had faith in him, opening her eyes as he told her to. And there he was, so beautiful in the golden glow of the bedside lamp, the concerned frown leaving his brow as her face lit up with happiness at the sight of him, and she launched herself against him, her arms about his neck as she clung to him.

'I don't know how you come to be here,' he spoke joyously into her hair, holding her just as tightly as she held him. 'But I do know I never want to let you go. Oh, God, Jade, I love you. I love you so much!'

She had known that, known it from the first. The words had never been spoken, but then they hadn't needed to be—every glance, every touch, every gesture had been full of love.

The kiss they shared was a rapturous delight, and Jade never wanted it to end. But of course it did, though not the warmth; that remained like a sunny day, bright and beautiful.

'I love you,' Jade told him ecstatically.

Light blazed in his eyes. 'I hoped as much when I walked into the room and found you waiting in my bed.'

She blinked. '*Your* bed?' she gasped. 'But— Penny.' She smiled tremulously at the other woman's machinations.

'Decided to give me an early Christmas present, did she?' David lovingly smoothed her hair back from her face, touching her cheek gently. 'I must remember to thank her,' he mused.

'We both must.' Jade gazed up at him glowingly.

'And to think I almost didn't come back here at all tonight,' he breathed softly. 'As it was, I left it until after midnight to arrive; I didn't feel in the mood for a party.'

'Neither did I,' she grimaced. 'But Penny made very sure that the only people we would see tonight was each other.'

David nodded. 'This was the room she gave me for the duration of my stay. If you had looked in the wardrobe and drawers you would have seen that I had left some of my clothes in them.'

She wished she had looked; at least knowing his things were there would have made her feel closer to him. 'Who would have guessed Penny is a romantic?' she teased.

David smiled. 'I'm just glad that she is.' He spoke huskily.

They kissed again, lingeringly, desire rising heatedly, neither able to stop touching the other in the wonder of their love.

'What made you change your mind and come back?'

Jade knew they had to talk, resting her head against David's shoulder as she drew in a ragged breath. 'Shadows,' she explained dully. 'David, there are some things about me that you don't know—— No, don't let me go just yet.' She clung to him as he would have moved back slightly so that he could look at her. 'After we've talked, you may not want to hold me again,' she told him tremulously.

'That won't happen,' he assured her softly, firmly. 'Not ever.'

She swallowed hard. 'Don't be so sure.' She quivered. 'I—the man who escaped from prison a couple of days ago—— That man, Peter Gifford, he——'

'Darling,' David cut in determinedly, 'I can't bear to see you putting yourself through this. Jade, I know who Peter Gifford is, and what he once was to you.'

'You can't!' she gasped, shaking her head in fierce denial.

'I do,' David insisted gently. 'Darling, I'm in publishing, and I take an active interest in all parts of it. Some of my best friends are newspaper magnates. But last of all,' he added softly, 'I know the Marshalls quite well.'

'Oh, God,' Jade choked, her face buried in her hands.

'Love, I realised who you were after you reacted so strangely to a couple of what I thought were harmless comments, began to question myself as to why that could be after you became really panicked the couple of times we saw police cars, and finally came up with the answer.'

'Then why did you continue to love me?' she cried in distress. 'How *could* you?'

'Jade, you only have to be seen in the company of children for it to be obvious you couldn't have been involved in hurting one the way Selina was,' he told her firmly. 'But I couldn't tell you that I knew the truth, I was frightened that would drive you away from me altogether.'

Jade looked up at him slowly, afraid to believe, and yet so desperately wanting to. The love she had always seen in his eyes for her hadn't diminished in the slightest, still darkening his eyes to navy blue, clear and strong, unreserved.

'I didn't know Peter intended—I had no idea he—I never would have——'

'Darling, I know that, whatever happened, you weren't involved in it,' David interrupted forcefully. 'Just as I'm sure the police do; they just have to cover all their options, unfortunately. Darling, I'll understand if you don't want to talk about any of it,' he reassured her gruffly. 'But if you do want to tell me I'll gladly listen—for your sake, not mine,' he added firmly. 'I don't need any more reassurances.'

And so Jade told him, every revealing, heart-rending, foolish detail.

'My poor darling,' he rasped once she had finished, his arms tight about her. 'Left with no one to turn to——'

'Don't pity me.' She shook her head. 'Selina was the one who was hurt.'

'Yes, she was.' David nodded, not even trying to dispute or gloss over that fact. 'But the scarring you have is just as deep, if of a different kind. And to think I believed you must still be in love with the bastard, that you had returned to London in the belief that he would contact you and the two of you could go away together!'

Jade gasped at that. 'I hate him, blame myself for ever being taken in by him!'

'Love can make fools of us all.' David sighed heavily. 'If I hadn't been hurting so much at your rejection of me I might have realised that, far from looking forward to seeing Gifford again, you were actually frightened. Jade,' he framed her face with gentle hands, 'will you marry me, live with me, be my beautiful, beloved wife?'

'But your friends? The Marshalls——'

'My friends will all love you. And I'm sure the Marshalls never believed you were involved in Selina's kidnapping. I remember them saying what a favourite you were with her, how she turned to you even more once she came back to school.'

Yes, Selina had clung to her quite considerably once she had been returned to her parents and had come back to school a few weeks later, but that had only made Jade's feelings of guilt all the deeper once she'd learnt the truth.

She didn't want David to suffer socially because he had married her.

'Darling, don't cross bridges before you come to them.' He smoothed the frown from between her eyes. 'And we're going to pay your parents a visit and tell them of our engagement. Don't be too hasty to judge them either, Jade,' he told her firmly as she would have interrupted. 'I think you were just too sensitive at the time, may have misjudged their reaction to what had happened. There could have been any number of reasons for their sudden lack of a social life, but the one that springs to mind the most is the fact that they may have wanted to devote all their time and love to you, to protecting you. The fact that they watched you only shows that they were concerned. Whatever, Jade, we will go and see them, there's nothing to be lost by doing that. And if they care about you, as I believe they do, then they're probably worried out of their minds about you.'

Whether he was right or not, she knew she could face what had to come. With David at her side she could face anything.

'In the meantime,' he drawled softly, 'at least I don't have to wonder any more what will be in my bed Christmas morning; it will be you, and every other morning of our lives, too!'

It sounded wonderful. Heaven.

But just before she sank into his arms, another thought popped into her mind. 'You still haven't explained completely about Christi and Dizzy,' she frowned.

His soft chuckle, before his mouth claimed hers, was full of wickedly mischievous humour...

'Gently,' David said sharply. 'Careful of her head,' he advised softly, for all the world as if Jade's mother had never held a baby in her arms before.

Jade shared a humorous smile at David's expense with two of the women who had stood as godmothers to Lia Sara, Christi and Dizzy returning the smile as they all watched the indulgent father as he fussed over his three-month-old daughter.

Lia Sara had been born exactly nine months to the day after Christmas Day, a tiny, red-haired, and now green-eyed, bundle of mischief, who her father had claimed was his last Christmas gift to Jade!

Christmas Eve one year later had seemed an ideal day for their daughter's christening, with Lia having four godmothers: Christi, Dizzy, Cathy and Penny, and four godfathers too: Lucas and Zach, Dominic and Simon.

David had lost no time after their wonderful Christmas together the year before in introducing her to his friends Christi and Dizzy. That was when Jade had learnt that when he had called them friends that was exactly what he had meant, the other two women both the proud mothers of young babies, their husbands, Lucas and Zach, two of the most attractive men—David excluded, of course!— Jade had ever met.

Lucas could seem a little daunting at first, unapproachable, until you saw the unashamed love in his eyes for his young wife, and then he became as humanly vulnerable and likeable as the rest of them.

The other couple, Dizzy and Zach, on the surface, were the most ill-matched pair imaginable, Dizzy so bubbly and flamboyant, Zach a staid professor of history, obligatory pipe, tweed jacket and all! But beneath Dizzy's outgoing nature was a sensitivity and vulnerability that her husband was completely attuned to. And the myth about Zach himself was completely shattered when David introduced him as Claudia Laurence, the author of all those passionate historical novels! No wonder David had been so amused when he promised to introduce Jade to 'her'!

In a very short time the other couples had become Jade's close friends too, until Jade wondered how she could ever have doubted she would fit into David's world.

Guests of honour today at Lia's christening were Jade's own parents, to whom, through David's help and understanding, she was now closer than ever. And the other guest of honour was Judy Maxwell. Sara's mother had become an honorary 'grandmother' to little Lia, she and Jade having formed a warm understanding that they had both felt from their first introduction. Maybe Sara really did approve of the love Jade and David shared...

Thank you, Sara, Jade offered up a silent prayer to the other woman on this day when all was so very right with her own world, knowing Sara wouldn't begrudge her that happiness; rather, she would rejoice in it.

Jade smiled tremulously as her gaze met David's across the room, their love passing between them like an electric shock.

Electrified satin, his eyes promised for later.

And Jade knew, beyond a shadow of a doubt, that she would always have David's love. As he would always have hers. And that love would always keep the shadows at bay.

Harlequin Presents

Coming Next Month

Available in January wherever paperback books are sold, or through Harlequin Reader Service:

In the U.S.
901 Fuhrmann Blvd.
P.O. Box 1397
Buffalo, N.Y. 14240-1397

In Canada
P.O. Box 603
Fort Erie, Ontario
L2A 5X3

CHRISTMAS IS FOR KIDS

Spend this holiday season with nine very special children. Children whose wishes come true at the magical time of Christmas.

Read American Romance's CHRISTMAS IS FOR KIDS— heartwarming holiday stories in which children bring together four couples who fall in love. Meet:

Frank, Dorcas, Kathy, Candy and Nicky—They become friends at St. Christopher's orphanage, but they really want to be adopted and become part of a real family, in #321 *A Carol Christmas* by Muriel Jensen.

Patty—She's a ten-year-old certified genius, but she wants what every little girl wishes for: a daddy of her own, in #322 *Mrs. Scrooge* by Barbara Bretton.

Amy and Flash—Their mom is about to deliver their newest sibling any day, but Christmas just isn't the same now—not without their dad. More than anything they want their family reunited for Christmas, in #323 *Dear Santa* by Margaret St. George.

Spencer—Living with his dad and grandpa in an all-male household has its advantages, but Spence wants Santa to bring him a mommy to love, in #324 *The Best Gift of All* by Andrea Davidson.

These children will win your hearts as they entice—and matchmake—the adults into a true romance. This holiday, invite them—and the four couples they bring together—into your home.

Look for all four CHRISTMAS IS FOR KIDS books available now from Harlequin American Romance. And happy holidays!

Step into a world of pulsing adventure, gripping emotion and lush sensuality with these evocative love stories penned by today's best-selling authors in the highest romantic tradition. Pursuing their passionate dreams against a backdrop of the past's most colorful and dramatic moments, our vibrant heroines and dashing heroes will make history come alive for you.

Watch for two new Harlequin Historicals each month, available wherever Harlequin books are sold. History was never so much fun—you won't want to miss a single moment!

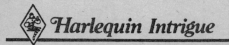

Harlequin Intrigue

Two exciting new stories each month.

Each title mixes a contemporary, sophisticated romance with the surprising twists and turns of a puzzler...romance with "something more."

Because romance can be quite an adventure.

Intrg-1

Romance, Suspense and Adventure

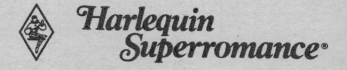

Harlequin Superromance®

LET THE GOOD TIMES ROLL...

Add some Cajun spice to liven up your New Year's celebrations and join Superromance for a romantic tour of the rich Acadian marshlands and the legendary Louisiana bayous.

Starting in January 1990, we're launching CAJUN MELODIES, a three-book tribute to the fun-loving people who've enriched America by introducing us to crawfish étouffé and gumbo, zydeco music and the Saturday night party, the *fais-dodo*. And learn about loving, Cajun-style, as you meet the tall, dark, handsome men who win their ladies' hearts with a beautiful, haunting melody....

Book One: *Julianne's Song*, January 1990
Book Two: *Catherine's Song*, February 1990
Book Three: *Jessica's Song*, March 1990

Indulge a Little
Give a Lot

An irresistible opportunity to pamper yourself with free gifts (plus proofs-of-purchase and postage and handling) and help raise up to $100,000.00 for **Big Brothers/Big Sisters Programs and Services** in Canada and the United States.

Each specially marked ''Indulge A Little'' Harlequin or Silhouette book purchased during October, November and December contains a proof-of-purchase that will enable you to qualify for luxurious gifts. And, for every specially marked book purchased during this limited time, Harlequin/Silhouette will donate 5¢ toward **Big Brothers/Big Sisters Programs and Services**, for a maximum contribution of $100,000.00.

For details on how you can indulge yourself, look for information at your favorite retail store or send a self-addressed stamped envelope to:

INDULGE A LITTLE
P.O. Box 618
Fort Erie, Ontario
L2A 5I3

ONE PROOF OF PURCHASE

To collect your free gift you must include the necessary number of proofs-of- purchase, plus postage and handling, along with the offer certificate available in retail stores or from the above address.

CHP-3

Harlequin®/Silhouette®